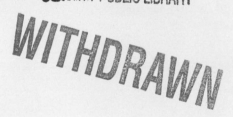

BORN
FOR EACH OTHER

BORN
FOR EACH
OTHER

•

Darlene Gardner

AVALON BOOKS
NEW YORK

PRINTED IN THE UNITED STATES OF AMERICA
ON ACID-FREE PAPER
BY HADDON CRAFTSMEN, BLOOMSBURG, PENNSYLVANIA

To Reva and Clay, my niece and nephew,
who inspired this book by being born just eight days apart.

Thanks to Deanna Hofmann and Elaine Sweitzer,
park naturalists at the Piney Run Nature Center
in Sykesville, Maryland,
for showing me their raptor mews and sharing stories
about their jobs.

Prologue

"I swear, in all my days, I've never seen a couple more in love than Annie and Michael," Rose Kubek declared as her daughter flailed at the air while reaching out for her best friend's son.

She missed his hand, but connected with the side of his nearly bald head. In return, she got a goofy, open-mouthed grin.

"I'm not sure babies can be in love," Christine Reeves said, scrunching up her forehead. "I think they have to develop motor control first."

"Nonsense." Rose peered over the side of the whitewashed crib at the two children, who were lying with their heads cocked at right angles so they were facing. "They have as strong a connection as you and me. They weren't born on the same day for nothing."

1

"Don't remind me." Christine sniffled, blinking the tears from her eyes. "I can't believe Michael and I won't be here to celebrate with you and Annie when they turn three months old on Sunday."

"You married a man whose lifelong dream was to serve in the military, Christine. You knew you'd have to leave someday."

"Of course I knew," Christine said as she swallowed a sob, "but I didn't expect the Air Force to send him on a three-year assignment to Norway. Oh, Rosie, what are we going to do without you and Annie?"

"You're going to do just fine," Rose answered, wiping away a tear. "The last I heard, they had telephones in Oslo."

"But it won't be the same." Christine flung herself into her best friend's arms. "We haven't been apart since you punched Sammy Evans in the nose for me in kindergarten."

"He shouldn't have made fun of your lisp. Even if you did used to call him Thtupid Thammy," Rose muttered an instant before delighted baby gurgles drew the women's attention to the crib. The babies had managed to inch closer to each other. They were smiling, and their arms were windmilling. The smell of baby powder filled the air.

"We can't let this separation tear them apart," Rose said gravely, "when destiny has decreed they should be together."

The women were silent for long minutes, watching their infants watch each other. The ticks of a clown-faced clock were the only sounds in the nursery aside from the soft coos and squeals coming from inside the crib.

"There's only one sensible thing to do," Rose said. "We'll betroth them to each other."

"That's a lovely thought," Christine said, but her smile was sad. "Except it's not practical."

"Don't tell me it's not practical. Babies are betrothed in Asia and Africa all the time. And they're not even in love like Annie and Michael."

"But how would we make the betrothal official?" Christine worried her bottom lip with her teeth. "How would we make it stick?"

Rose thought for a minute. "Remember the pacts we made when we were little girls? Remember how we sealed them?"

Christine nodded, and then breathed the words as though they were magical. "The pinky link."

Rose extended her smallest finger as though getting ready to sip from a cup of tea. After a slight hesitation, Christine did the same. Their eyes linked at the same moment as their pinkies.

"Pact," the women intoned in unison.

"Let's just hope that someday Michael and Annie understand why we did what we've done," Christine said.

"Look at them," Rose said. Inside the crib, the squealing infants had managed to link their tiny hands. Baby Michael's green eyes didn't stray from baby Annie's brown ones. Their pinky fingers were wrapped securely around each other. "If that's not love, I don't know what is. How could they not realize they were born for each other?"

Chapter One

Justifiable matricide.

Annie Kubek figured no jury would convict after learning she'd been forced to endure nearly twenty-five years of hearing she'd met her future husband while wearing diapers.

"Can you believe it, Annie? The day we've been waiting for is finally here." Rose Kubek was bent over the oven, wearing an oversized red-and-white mitt and checking on the progress of her stuffed cabbage rolls. A savory aroma reached Annie's nostrils. Okay. So she wouldn't kill her. Besides being a good cook, Rose was her mother. And, despite it all, Annie did love her.

"In just minutes," her mother continued, "you're going to become reacquainted with your fiancé."

Matricide might be out, but that didn't mean Annie couldn't take drastic steps to silence her. Maybe she should go shopping for a muzzle. The problem was where to find one. Muzzles 'R Us?

"Don't start that again, Mom." Although it went against her nature, Annie tried to remain calm. She really did. "Michael Reeves is not my fiancé. I don't even know the man."

"That's not true." Her mother peered into the various pots simmering on the stove. She was wearing her Sunday best, a navy dress with a flared skirt that hid spreading hips. Her graying hair was neatly done in a beauty-shop special. "The two of you fell in love before he moved away from Elmwood."

Annie rolled her eyes so dramatically they nearly disappeared in back of her head. Calmness be danged. She was being provoked here. Yet again.

"He moved away from Elmwood when we were infants!" Annie threw up her hands. "We wore diapers. We passed the time by drooling. Neither of us could even sit up."

"Sitting up is not a skill you need to fall in love," her mother said. She could be as intractable as a tick on a raccoon, Annie thought. Once she had her mind set on something, she wouldn't budge.

"I don't know why you have to be so stubborn about this," her mother continued. "By fighting destiny, you're banging your head against the clouds. The fight's so useless you don't even get the satisfaction of a headache."

Annie closed her eyes, thinking her mother was wrong. Tiny little women who were replicas of Rose

Kubek were inside her head, hammering away. "You can't know how ridiculous you sound."

"Ridiculous? Think about this, Annie, Michael wouldn't be in Elmwood if you weren't fated to be together."

"Michael is visiting Elmwood because his mother lives here!" Annie protested.

"Well, then, Christine wouldn't have moved back to Elmwood if destiny hadn't decided it wanted Michael right here beside you."

"I give up," Annie said, throwing up her hands. She was uncomfortably aware that every time they had this conversation, it ended the same way.

Her mother turned from the stove and really looked at Annie for the first time since she'd entered the kitchen five minutes ago. "Oh, dear," she said, clutching at her chest, her face contorted in horror. "I didn't realize you were wearing *that*."

Annie looked down at her ensemble, which consisted of a standard-issue outfit of forest-green belted trousers, sensible black shoes, and short-sleeved, button-down tan shirt. Remembering where she was, she removed her wide-brimmed matching hat from her head. "I'm a park naturalist, Mom. This is how we dress. What's wrong with it?"

"If you're Smokey the Bear fighting forest fires, nothing." She crossed the kitchen and stood in front of Annie, plucking twigs and leaves from short, dark hair that curled haphazardly. "But since you're trying to make a good impression on your fiancé, everything."

"I'm not trying to—"

"If you hurry," her mother interrupted, "you might have time to run along to your place and put on something pretty."

The sing-song of the doorbell rang out. Annie smiled and settled her hands on her lean hips.

"Too late now," she said and strode to the front door. The sooner she opened it and laughed in the face of the fate her mother was always talking about, the better.

Her younger brother Joe was moving toward the door, but he stopped when he saw Annie and made a gesture indicating she should precede him.

"Since it's your intended out there, it's only right you should answer it," he teased, his mouth twitching in amusement.

"Remind me to spray you with shaving cream later," she said dryly, referring to a favored prank from their childhood.

"Now, now," he drawled, crossing his arms over his chest and raising his dark brows. "Wouldn't that be a little childish for a lady who's one step from the altar?"

Annie scowled at him and continued on her path, aware that her father had also come to watch the show. She pasted on a smile, which wasn't difficult considering Christine Reeves was beaming at her from the other side of the screen door. Mrs. Reeves had come to live in Elmwood six months before, a widow determined to start a new life. She was one of the sweetest, classiest women Annie knew.

It helped tremendously that Mrs. Reeves had never once mentioned Annie was destined to marry her son.

She hadn't even showed her any pictures, the way Rose used to when Annie was growing up. It got Annie to wondering whether her mother had dreamed up this betrothal nonsense all by herself.

"Annie, dear. It's so good to see you," Mrs. Reeves said, hobbling through the screen door and greeting Annie's brother and father just as warmly. She was using crutches and her left leg was encased in a cast she hadn't been wearing a few days before. Before Annie could ask about it, Mrs. Reeves turned with a look of unmistakable pride to the man who had trailed into the house behind her. "I'd like you to meet my son Michael. Michael, this is Frank Kubek and his children, Joe and Annie."

Annie looked at Michael Reeves and promptly forgot about Mrs. Reeves's cast. She'd refused to examine a photograph of him in years, but the boyhood depictions she had seen didn't prepare her for the flesh-and-blood article. She examined him as he greeted her family, and her phony smile turned genuine.

Annie put great stock in first impressions, and Michael had cultured city boy written all over him.

He was tall, probably at least six-feet-one, with the type of lean musculature that would make him the perfect model for any clothes he happened to put on. His were expensive: charcoal-gray tailored trousers with a lighter gray button-down shirt rolled up at the sleeves to reveal sturdy forearms dusted with golden hair. Matching suede oxfords completed the pulled-together picture.

His face was just as impressive as his ensemble. His

thick blond hair was expertly cut and swept back from a high, wide forehead that drew attention to startling green eyes. They were framed by surprisingly thick brown lashes most women would die for. His nose was straight, his chin strong, his cheekbones high.

When he turned toward Annie, his mouth curved in a smile so dazzling he could have been a pitchman in a toothpaste commercial. Annie bit her bottom lip, trying to control the amusement bubbling there. But she couldn't stop it from spreading to her eyes.

"It's a pleasure to meet you, Annie," he said, like the perfect gentleman he undoubtedly was. "My mother has been talking about your family for so many years I feel like I already know you."

His diction was perfect, his accent nonexistent, his tone low and rich. Annie struggled valiantly to contain the laughter that had been threatening to escape since he'd walked into the house.

"You, too," she managed to say.

All her mother's talk about her fate being inexorably intertwined with Michael Reeves's fate had been made even more ludicrous.

As though a park naturalist who counted camping and kayaking as her hobbies could ever marry a man who looked as though he'd stepped straight out of the pages of *GQ*.

Marry him! Annie wouldn't even been able to take him seriously.

The destiny her mother was always talking about was not destined to be!

* * *

Michael Reeves brought a thick piece of homemade rye bread to his mouth and tore off a chunk with his teeth, hoping the act of chewing would hide his scowl.

He'd been taught from an early age to hide his feelings, especially when they were negative. Usually that wasn't a problem, but he'd never met a woman who irked him more than Annie Kubek.

Aside from when his mother told the story of how she'd broken her leg slipping on a banana peel, Annie's eyes had been sparkling with amusement all evening. Especially when they alighted on him.

Because he didn't grasp what was so funny, he couldn't have been more irritated had a rampaging virus devoured his computer files. She'd even taken his mind off how his mother was going to cope with a broken leg when he lived too far away to help.

"You're abnormally quiet today, Annie." Mrs. Kubek drummed her fingers on the well-used oak of the dining room table. "Don't you have anything you want to ask Michael?"

Annie gave her mother a beatific smile. It confounded Michael that the masculine lines of her uniform and the short, boyish cut of her curly hair didn't render her unattractive. Instead, he thought darkly, she was lovely. Her nose had a slightly turned-up end, and her cheeks a natural rosy glow. Her skin was dewy and unblemished, and her laughing eyes were a very pretty brown shot through with streaks of gold.

"It's been hard to talk with my mouth so full of your wonderful stuffed cabbage," Annie said, unwillingly drawing Michael's gaze to her mouth. Her mouth was wide and her lips were full, but not too full. She wasn't wearing lipstick, but she didn't need any. Like her cheeks, her lips looked like they had been dipped in a vat of rosy color. "You outdid yourself this time, Mom. They're delicious."

Instead of acknowledging the compliment, Mrs. Kubek glowered at her daughter, Michael feared he was wearing a similar glower. Not that he wanted to answer any questions Annie had, he told himself firmly. Still, it would have been nice if those luscious lips had wanted something from him. Even if it were only an answer.

"Christine tells us you were educated all over Europe," Frank Kubek cut in, and Michael was grateful to have something to take his mind off the irritating brunet somebody had callously seated directly across from him. "That must have been exciting."

Michael forced himself to smile. His international education had shaped the man he was, but in truth constantly switching curriculums had been a hardship. He wasn't about to say so. His mother had enough guilt about dragging him across Europe without him adding to it.

"It *was* exciting," he said, letting his eyes touch his mother's. He knew he didn't imagine the relief he saw there. "How many children have the opportunity to study in Korea, Italy, Greece, and Germany? How many Americans get to attend Michigan State University while living in Aachen?"

"Aachen? Isn't that in Germany?" Annie entered the conversation for one of the few times that evening. Michael looked levelly at her and nodded, willing himself not to sound defensive. Although he wasn't exactly sure what he should be defensive about.

"Yes. Michigan State has a campus there. It's west of Koln on the Belgian border. That's where I got my engineering degree."

Annie's smile grew so wide he swore he could see her molars. Unfortunately, she even had nice molars.

"That must mean you're bilingual."

"The instruction was in English, Annie, but Michael wouldn't have had a problem if it had been in German," his mother cut in, smiling at him in that indulgent way she had. "He has a knack for languages. He's fluent in German and French, and he can speak some Italian."

"How very cosmopolitan," Annie remarked.

Michael *was* cosmopolitan. He belonged in a city where excitement and opportunities abounded, not in a rural community like Elmwood. He wouldn't even be here if his mother hadn't broken her leg. But the way Annie pronounced the word cosmopolitan made it sound like an insult.

"I hear you work at CompTech headquarters in Los Angeles." Even though he was dark-haired and dark-eyed like his sister, Joe Kubek was the anti-Annie. That was to say, he was friendly and personable. "I'm impressed. Anyone who knows computers knows CompTech is a major player. What exactly do you do there?"

"I'm in hardware development, so a big part of my job is keeping abreast of the market," Michael said, trying his best not to look at Annie. "I can do much of that in California, but I spend a lot of time traveling to seminars and trade shows."

"You mean," Annie interjected, a corner of her mouth lifting, "that you spend a lot of time wining and dining and being wined and dined. Schmoozing and being schmoozed."

Since his job description could have included a clause about impressing potential clients and weeding out the good sales pitches from the bad, her portrayal was essentially accurate. If her eyes hadn't been bright with amusement, he might not have found it objectionable.

Michael forced himself to smile at her even though it hurt his lips. "Anybody with a business degree knows networking is as important as know-how."

"A business degree?" One of Annie's eyebrows shot up. "I thought you had an engineering degree."

"He has both, dear," his mother said. "The company was so impressed with Michael that they helped pay for his master's degree at Stanford. He's on track to become one of the youngest vice presidents Comp-Tech has ever had. His father, rest his soul, couldn't have been prouder. He reached the rank of general himself, you know."

Michael flushed a little, but it was in annoyance rather than embarrassment. His single-minded ambition to advance in his field, once applauded by his successful father, was well-known among his friends and coworkers. This was the first time anyone had found it amusing.

"That's fantastic." Joe, at least, was more impressed

than amused. "It makes what I do look like small potatoes."

"That's not true, Joe." Mrs. Kubek stopped slanting her daughter disapproving glances long enough to address her son. "You have a perfectly good job in the technical services department at the junior college. And what about those software programs you're designing?"

"*Trying* to design," Joe interjected. "They have more than a few kinks I can't seem to work out."

"If you like, I'll take a look at them while I'm here," Michael offered.

"Would you really do that? Gee, thanks."

"Don't mention it," Michael said uncomfortably. The truth was that he found software design so enticing that Joe would be doing him the favor rather than the other way around.

"You're such a fabulous cook that it must have been a joy to grow up in your family, Mrs. Kubek," he said, as much to change the subject as because it was true.

"And you're a charming guest," Mrs. Kubek said, glowing as brightly as the lights in the overhead chandelier. "But you haven't tasted the best part yet. Annie, would you get the plum cake?"

Michael watched her go, but he wasn't thinking about dessert. His eyes took in her graceful figure, and he wondered what she would look like in more feminine clothes. He scowled as she disappeared into the kitchen and reached for another piece of bread, but every morsel was already gone. He composed his face.

"It's a shame Annie doesn't have a date for her cousin Walter's wedding this Saturday," Mrs. Kubek said on a sigh. Because this was the third time she'd mentioned her dateless daughter and the wedding, Michael figured it must be weighing on her mind.

She smiled at him, and he smiled back. Surely Mrs. Kubek must realize why her daughter was dateless. If Annie treated all single men the way she'd been treating him, no wonder nobody wanted to go out with her.

Mrs. Kubek gazed across the table at his mother, who shrugged. What that exchange meant, Michael didn't have a clue. Then Annie, still with that maddening curve to her lips, returned with plum cake. For a while, nobody said anything at all.

Michael knew the cake must be good, but Annie's nonsensical reaction to him had him so irritated he could have been eating sand. He'd been sincere when he complimented Mrs. Kubek on her cooking, and the fact that he wasn't enjoying her plum cake annoyed him even more.

He wanted to get to know the Kubeks better, to make sure they could provide his mother with the support he wouldn't be able to give her when he was all the way across the country. But that was going to have to wait until he made Annie Kubek pay for the way she'd been silently laughing at him.

When he finished the cake, he put down his fork and thanked Mrs. Kubek. Then, after having his offer to clear the table refused, he announced he was in the mood for a walk.

"The only problem is that I don't know my way around." He deliberately stared straight at Annie and gave her his best smile. "Annie, would you join me?"

"Me?" She pointed at her chest and widened her

eyes before shaking her head. "I couldn't possibly leave my mother in the lurch with all these dishes to do."

"You can if I say you can, and I say you can." Mrs. Kubek was smiling for one of the first times that evening. "Joe will help me clear the table."

"And I'll keep Rosie company while she works," his mother piped in. "You two just run along and have a good time."

Annie's eyes swung to her brother. "You'll come too, won't you, Joe?"

"Can't." His smile was bigger than his reply warranted. "Didn't you hear Mom? I'm helping her clean up. Besides, you probably want to get better acquainted with Michael anyway. Don't you, sis?"

"Well, uh, of course," Annie stammered. Her gaze ping-ponged to her father, and Michael could see that the plea for help was still in her eyes. "How about you, Dad? Are you up for a walk?"

"Thanks for the invitation, Annie," Frank Kubek said in a soft voice at odds with his appearance. He was big and burly, his dominant feature a pair of sharply arching eyebrows that made him look deceptively ferocious. "But there's an article on fly-fishing I've been wanting to read."

Annie closed her eyes briefly before she looked at Michael across the table. She smiled, but it was a counterfeit smile. She was well and truly snared, and she knew it. Like a mouse that couldn't wriggle its way out of a trap. Still, she gave another tug.

"There aren't many streetlights around here," she

said, and he thought her voice had lost momentum. "And fewer sidewalks."

"There's a full moon," Rose Kubek pointed out, "and some parkland nearby you're always saying is the perfect place for a walk."

"Walking in those city shoes won't be very comfortable," Annie interjected.

"I'm sure I can manage." Michael stood, his smile still in place. His jaw ached from the effort of keeping it there, but he reminded himself it was only a few more minutes until he had some answers. He looked at Annie. "Shall we go?"

Chapter Two

The night air was just cool enough that Annie wished she had worn a jacket. Michael walked at her side, his hands jammed in his pockets, navigating the path easily even though his shoes were all wrong. He looked as perfectly cosmopolitan as he had when he'd walked through the door. Men like him probably perpetually maintained the ideal body temperature, neither too hot nor too cold.

Annie took in the familiar countryside as they walked. This corner of western Pennsylvania was like a slice of paradise that had been laid out by God's loving hand in the valley between two mountains.

The houses were spaced far enough apart that neighbors could be neighborly without crowding one another. Traffic was light, and the stars were so numerous the moonlit sky gave the impression of a piece of black velvet sprinkled with tiny diamonds. A brook babbled nearby, and the smells of spring blossoms filled the air.

The beauty was so abundant that Annie wondered how Christine Reeves could have left it all those years ago for her military husband. To Annie, leaving a home she loved was a sacrifice no woman should ever be asked to make.

Hoo-ah. Hoo-ah.

They had just stepped onto the walking trail that wound around the small park when somewhere above them, in a tall tree, came a distinctive call. Annie stopped dead, momentarily forgetting the man at her side, concentrating only on the call of the barred owl. With a passion only she had ever been able to understand, she wanted to see as well as hear it. She pursed her lips and let out a long, monotonous trill.

"Rrrrrrrrrrrrrrrr."

"What are you doing?" A few steps beyond her, Michael whirled, his eyes as round as that of the barred owl she was trying to call in. "Because, I've got to tell you, this whistling at me doesn't make any sense after the way you acted at dinner."

"Shhhh. I'm not whistling at you," she said impatiently, silencing the question on his lips but not in his eyes. She didn't have time for explanations. She took a breath and trilled again.

"Rrrrrrrrrrrrrrrr."

She heard the flapping of the barred owl's wings moments before she saw him in the moonlight, a chunky, brown-eyed creature with dark barring on his upper breast and dark streaking below. As always, the sight of one of the birds flying gracefully through the sky filled her with a sense of nature's power.

"How'd you do that?" Michael asked, following the path of the owl before it disappeared back into the woods. It was a moment before Annie, still feeling the rush of seeing a bird of prey in the wild, could answer.

"Park-naturalist training," she said finally. Michael stared at her, obviously waiting for more of an explanation. Flippancy, evidently, wouldn't get her anywhere with him. Not that she wanted to go anywhere. "I could tell it was a barred owl from its call, so I imitated the sound an Eastern screech owl makes. The barred owl hunts the screech owl, so naturally it came out to investigate."

"Do you break into whistles often?" he asked, effectively killing the magic of the moment when the owl made its grand emergence from the cover of the trees.

"It wasn't a whistle. It was a trill," Annie snapped. "And I don't trill often. Sometimes I shriek. Other times I bark, growl, or screech."

She continued walking, more briskly this time, wishing she could have flown away with the owl. At best, its appearance had been a momentary diversion.

Perhaps she hadn't been fair to snap at Michael, but she hadn't liked the look in his eyes when he'd asked her to take this walk. It was too bold. Too daring. She still thought it was laughable that her mother was under the delusion that Michael Reeves was her soul mate, but now that she had to deal with him she no longer felt like laughing.

They walked for long minutes in a silence she had no intention of breaking, and she relaxed marginally. Hopefully, he was the strong, silent type who only spoke when spoken to. In her experience, men who looked like he did were rarely confrontational.

"So," he said conversationally, "suppose you tell me what it is about me that you find so funny."

Annie blinked. The chill she had felt when they started the walk was a distant memory. Instead, she felt as though he'd just tossed her in the fire and dared her to come out unscathed. So much for her theory about his non-confrontational personality.

"Funny?" she asked, bluffing to buy herself time. She scuffed one of her feet in the packed earth that made up the walking trail. "What makes you think I find anything about you funny?"

"It was a pretty big tip-off when I walked through the door and you could barely keep from laughing."

Too late, Annie realized the consequences of her behavior. She hadn't meant to insult him, but the edge to his voice told her that's exactly what she'd done. She frowned, because Michael's only offense was that he had curried her mother's favor as husband material. She gave a stab at excusing the inexcusable.

"I was remembering a joke somebody told me earlier today," she said.

"What was the joke?"

Annie bit her lip, because at that moment every joke she'd ever been told had flown out of her head as swiftly as the owl had disappeared from sight.

"I knew it," he said when she didn't immediately answer. He shook his head as they walked from under the cover of the trees, and the moonlight caught the golden hues in his hair. "There was no joke. You were just making that up."

"I was not," Annie said indignantly. "The people I work with at the nature center have terrific senses of humor."

He pinned her with a look, and she felt like a fly caught in a web. Why, oh why, had she let herself be hoodwinked into taking this walk with him? She quickened her pace, but he kept up with her effortlessly, and she knew there was no getting away from him. Just as the fly couldn't escape the spider.

"If you weren't making it up, tell me the joke."

"Okay." She gulped, squared her shoulders, and desperately searched her brain until she came up with something. "What does an educated owl say?"

He shrugged.

"Whom," she said.

The corners of his mouth lifted before something obviously occurred to him to make them turn down. "I admit that's amusing, but it's not laugh-out-loud funny."

"I wasn't laughing out loud," Annie pointed out. "I was chuckling silently to myself."

The night was unusually quiet, Annie thought as they continued to walk. There wasn't another soul on the trail, and the nocturnal animals seemed to be eavesdropping to determine whether she could extract herself from the predicament her twisted sense of humor had put her into.

"Okay, then," Michael said after a moment. Annie could tell from the tone of his voice that he wasn't going to let go of the subject just yet. "For sake of argument, let's say I accept your totally unbelievable story about the joke making you laugh."

"I thought we were arguing that you believed my story," she argued. "When you call my story totally unbelievable, it doesn't sound as though you're saying you believe it."

He blew out a breath that ruffled the strands of his blond hair and gave it a faintly mussed quality. If anything, the touch of imperfection enhanced his classic good looks.

"Could we just move on to the next question?" he asked.

"That depends upon what the next question is."

"Why did you look so amused all through dinner every time I said anything?"

"I don't like that question. Let's go on to the next one."

"There is no next one." Michael sounded annoyed. "I don't know why you're having so much trouble giving me a straight answer. If I could sit through dinner with you smirking at me, I figure that at the very least I deserve an answer."

"I wasn't smirking," Annie protested. "I was smiling."

"It was a smile with smirkish undertones."

Annie frowned at him. "I don't think smirkish is a word."

"I don't care if it's a word or not. All I care about is that you're avoiding my question."

"I already forgot what it was."

He let out an exasperated breath. "Why did you spend the evening smirking at everything I said?"

Annie sighed. Whatever had possessed her to think of him as non-confrontational? He had securely sunk his talons into his prey, and he wasn't about to relinquish his hold. Unfortunately, she was his prey.

"What are you," she muttered, "a flesh-eating eagle?"

"Since I'm waiting for an answer to my question, I'm not going to ask what you mean," he said, and Annie knew she was beaten. The only recourse remaining was to tell him the truth and hope his sense of humor was as refined as hers.

"If you really must know . . ." she began and trailed off, still not wanting to tell him. The path was all shadows and light, but now they were free of the trees again, and she felt terribly exposed.

"I must know," he said firmly.

"Okay," she all but shouted. He was getting to her. Criminy, he'd already gotten to her, which made her more blunt than usual. "I was laughing because I'd sooner marry that barred owl we just saw than you. We'd make a better match."

He gave her a look that was a mixture of incomprehension and, she thought, annoyance.

"I don't get it," he said, shaking his head. "Not the part about you matching up with an owl, which I understand just fine. I don't get why your first look at me made you think about marriage."

Annie let out an exasperated breath, wondering if he were this obtuse all the time. "Because of the pact," she said irritably.

His eyebrows, which were as perfect as the rest of him, rose. He looked well and truly confused.

"What pact?"

"Don't tell me you don't know about the pact?" Annie gazed at him with an expression of pure incredulity on her pretty face. Her voice had risen a full octave. "How could you not know about the pact?"

"At the risk of repeating myself," he said dryly, "what pact?"

She waved her hands in a gesture he already knew meant she was irritated. Since they'd begun the walk, she would have given a windmill keen competition in kicking up a breeze. "The pact our mothers made when we were babies. The one where they betrothed us to each other."

"Betrothed us?" he repeated, and then let out an incredulous laugh. "Let me get this straight. You're claiming our mothers promised when we were babies that we would marry one day?"

"I'm not claiming anything. That's what happened. They thought they were helping destiny along, because they have some harebrained notion we were born for each other. My mother even has an engagement picture of us."

He let out another hoot of laughter. "An 'engagement picture' of two babies?"

"Yes," she said crossly, folding her arms over her chest. "It's a photograph of the two of us lying next to each other in a crib. We're looking into each other's eyes and holding hands. If you don't believe me, I'll show it to you."

"Oh, I believe there's a photo," Michael said,

chuckling. "I just don't believe my mother would do anything like that. She's always let me make my own decisions. Are you sure she was involved in this . . . baby betrothal?"

"Sure, she was involved," Annie said, although she didn't sound quite convinced. She raised her chin a notch. "My mother told me they did a pinky link to seal the bargain."

"A pinky link?" Michael looked down at one of his own little fingers, and shook his head. "But that's ridiculous."

"That's what I think. Especially now that I've met you."

Her last remark had the same effect as a funeral director who walks into a comedy club. It killed the laughter percolating on his lips. He narrowed his eyes and stopped walking. She continued a few steps before she seemed to realize he was no longer abreast of her.

"What do you mean, now that you've met me?"

"Oh, come on, Michael." Annie peered at him over her shoulder. "That's why I kept laughing tonight. I mean, look at you. I don't have anything against marriage. Or men, for that matter. But I could never be with somebody like you."

"What's wrong with me?" he asked, knowing he sounded defensive but not caring. Why wouldn't she want to be with him?

"Nothing's *wrong* with you." She walked back to his side and looked up at him. The moonlight was so bright he could clearly see her earnest brown eyes. "I'm sure you're a perfectly nice guy, but you're not somebody I'd get involved with. You are most definitely not my type."

"Why not?" The words were clipped. Her candor, he thought, he could have done without.

"Why not?" Her eyes widened as though the answer should be obvious. "Do you want the short list or the long one?"

"You're saying there's more than one reason?"

She nodded. "There's a whole slew of reasons."

A whole slew of reasons? Michael's lips tightened, and his muscles clenched. To unclench them, he resumed their walk but quickened the pace. The packed earth of the walking trail wasn't altogether level, but she kept up with him easily. For some reason, that further irritated him.

As he walked, he vowed he was not, under any circumstance, going to ask her reasons again. He didn't want to know. What's more, anything she came up with wouldn't make a whit of difference.

"What reasons?" he heard himself asking.

"Well," she said slowly, consideringly, "we could start with your hair."

He reached up, touching the golden strands. He didn't need a haircut, because he had his hair trimmed regularly in deference to the socializing that was part of his job. His hand moved back to his scalp as he wondered whether he'd gone bald without realizing it. But all he felt was thick, springy hair.

"What's wrong with my hair?" he asked, and his voice cracked on the question.

"It's too short." She tilted her head as she turned and appraised him. She looked like she could have been a stylist at a beauty salon discussing what to do about his problem. "Too stylish. Too blond."

He hadn't given his hair much thought before that moment, but he could have sworn he remembered other women complimenting him on it. He certainly couldn't recall anyone else finding fault with it. His fingers dropped from his hair—his too-short, too-stylish, too-blond hair—to his side.

"So you're saying you prefer a man with long, messy dark hair?" he asked, disliking the little hitch in his voice.

"Messy's the wrong word. Rumpled would be more like it." She laughed, completely missing the fact that he hadn't meant his comment to be funny. "Let's move on to your face."

His hand moved to his cheek.

"It's too sculpted," she said, gazing at him critically. They were walking even more quickly now, but the increased exertion wasn't even making her breath come harder. "Your eyes are too green. Your nose too straight. Your cheekbones too high. Your profile too perfect."

"I hadn't realized those things were liabilities," he said, and he couldn't keep his mouth from slanting in irritation.

"They're not," Annie said easily, the smile still in her voice. "All together, they just make you look like an aristocrat. Don't get me wrong. Most women probably find you darling. I'm just talking about my personal preferences. For example, I personally think you're too tall. Other women like that in a man."

"Go on," he said, gritting his teeth.

"You walk too fast."

In answer, he stopped abruptly. She did too, looking up at him with laughing eyes. She laid a hand on his arm, as though something had just occurred to her. Warmth spread under her hand.

"Oh, here's one of the main ones. You're too cosmopolitan." His lips twisted, because this explained the comment she'd made at the table. "You're much too worldly for someone like me. I like the simple things in life, like backpacking and kayaking."

"What makes you think I don't?"

"C'mon, Michael. When was the last time you did either of those things?"

"I have a demanding job in the city. Opportunities for those sorts of things don't exactly abound."

"See," she said, wrinkling her nose at him as her hand dropped from his arm. "I knew it."

"Just because I don't make a habit of kayaking and backpacking doesn't mean I wouldn't like to," he muttered, but she continued talking as though she hadn't heard him.

"Here's another one." She almost sounded excited, as though she were getting into the spirit of things. "There's your job. I mean, computers. Come on."

"What's wrong with having a job working with computers?"

She held up her hands so he could see her palms. "Nothing. It's perfectly fine for someone else's boyfriend, but I don't want a high-tech man. Don't get me wrong. I realize the value of computers, and I don't have anything against them. But I'm not interested in them."

"So I'm too high-tech?"

"Uh-huh," she agreed. "And too ambitious."

"Too ambitious?" he sputtered, at a loss as to how anyone could find fault with such an admirable quality. "Impossible. A man can't be too ambitious."

"In my book, he can. After all, we're talking about my preferences."

She was silent for a moment, prompting him to ask, "Are you done?"

She thought for a moment. "I could go on, but I guess that about covers the main points."

"Let me see if I get this straight. You're taking exception to my hair, my height, my personality, my job, and my ambition."

"You left out your face," she reminded him.

"Of course." He threw up his hands. "How could I have forgotten to include my face?"

The annoyance he'd felt at dinner was nothing compared to the emotion surging through him now. She'd just cheerfully spelled out the multitude of reasons he didn't attract her. The problem was, for some unfathomable reason, she attracted him. Never mind that she was no more his type than he was hers. She trilled at owls. She dressed in men's clothing, and her hair, which was a mass of crazy loops, fell well short of her shoulders.

He liked his woman soft and sophisticated with long, straight hair. Michael frowned as it occurred to him that was the type of woman who usually sought him out. He'd never had to spend much time pursuing the opposite sex. He'd grown up in Europe, surrounded by beautiful women, and he'd been happy enough to let them pursue him.

His relationships had been uncommitted and uncomplicated, because he wanted them that way. He was far too busy for a serious relationship and far too ambitious to let any woman sidetrack him from his career goals.

Until Annie had told him all the things wrong with him, he'd been far too ambivalent to waste precious time on a woman who wasn't interested in him.

"Michael." Annie sounded hesitant for the first time. "I hope you didn't take anything I said personally. I wasn't making a list of your faults, you understand. I was simply listing the reasons you aren't my type."

"You made that perfectly clear," he said through clenched teeth.

"Oh, good," she said, smiling again. She had a lovely smile, wide and guileless. It made her candor all the more biting, because she'd obviously meant every word. "I'm glad we got that settled. Now we don't have to talk about it anymore."

"Actually," he said, thoughtfully scratching his chin. However unwittingly, she'd issued a challenge, and he intended to take it. "There is one more thing I was wondering about."

"What's that?"

"I was wondering how you feel about my kisses?"

Her eyes widened, not in fright, he was sure, but in confusion. The moonlight softened her features so she looked almost ethereal. Then she opened her mouth again, and the words that came out were anything but heavenly.

"Your kisses? Since I've never had one of your kisses, I'd have to say that I don't know. But my guess is they wouldn't be my type of kisses any more than the rest of you is my type of man."

That did it. If he'd had second thoughts about the wisdom of what he was about to do, her quick dismissal made him only more determined to prove her wrong. He put his hands on her shoulders, feeling the heat of her even through her thick ranger shirt, and bent his head down to hers. He breathed in the fresh scent of strawberry shampoo mingled with the cool sweetness of the air, and all of his blood seemed to leave his body so that he felt light-headed.

It was as if his brain had suddenly gone missing, because he had a sudden, overpowering *need* to kiss the lips that had thoroughly dismissed him. He wanted to believe the reason was nothing more complicated than the unconscious challenge she'd issued, but he already knew that it was.

"Are you going to kiss me?" she asked incredulously, her eyes mirroring her astonishment.

"That's the only way to find out whether my kisses fall into the same unacceptable category as the rest of me," he murmured the instant before he claimed her mouth.

At the feel of her soft mouth under his, he closed his eyes, trying to fight off the powerful sensations swirling through him. She was warm and womanly and somehow familiar, and he wondered idiotically whether the baby Michael had sneaked a kiss when they'd been alone in the crib.

He cupped the back of her head, drawing her closer

so he could mold his lips more securely to hers. For a moment, he was content to feel her lips clinging to his, her breath mingling with his own, her heart beating against his.

Wow, she could kiss. The thought ran haphazardly through his mind as she confirmed with her mouth that his kiss was making her forget all about her ridiculous assertion that he wasn't her type.

No woman could respond like this to a man who wasn't her type. And, oh, how he wanted to be her type.

Finally, Michael drew back from her and leaned his forehead weakly against hers. He willed his heartbeat to return to normal, but it wasn't cooperating. It was tripping so fast and beating so hard she could probably hear it. It was a long moment before he trusted himself to speak.

"So, what's the verdict on my kiss?" he asked, his lips curving, supremely confident of her answer.

"It wasn't bad," she said breezily, "but you're still not my type."

His head jerked up, convinced he hadn't heard her correctly. He examined her brown eyes, but he couldn't read a thing in them.

"What?"

"I said you're still not my type." She didn't sound anywhere near as breathless as he felt. "So I'm glad we got that kiss out of the way, because that proved it."

"Are you saying you didn't like the kiss?" he asked, even though that didn't compute. It was like inserting a Pentium chip into a computer and watching its speed decrease. He couldn't remember the last woman who had responded to him so thoroughly. Or the last woman who had affected him so deeply without half trying. "You weren't shaken?"

"Not shaken. Not stirred."

"Not shaken? Not stirred? Not bad?" he repeated, his ego thoroughly deflated. He couldn't stop himself from adding, "I thought it was a little better than not bad."

"It was agreeable, but you're no James Bond," she said cheekily. She tossed her head, and her short hair danced around her smiling face. "Like I said, it proved what I was saying before. You're not my type."

Michael refrained from asking if James Bond were her type. Or, more to the point, how a kiss that could have ignited swampland had proved any such thing. But he found he couldn't say anything at all.

"Let's be honest here. I'm not exactly your type either."

"Of course not," Michael said, finding his voice. He agreed more to save face than because he believed her. At the moment, he couldn't think of a single reason why she wasn't his type. Except that she was infuriating.

"I'm glad we got that settled, then." Her voice was so completely normal she could have been talking about the weather. "If you don't mind, I'd like to head back."

"Of course I don't mind," he said, turning in the direction from which they'd come. But, darn it, he did mind. Mere moments after informing him his kiss had been lacking, she'd effectively told him she'd had enough of his company.

Michael spent the ten minutes it took to walk to her parents' house trying to convince himself he should resist the urge to prove Annie Kubek wrong. He already found her more intriguing than the computers he worked on, a statement he'd never been able to make about any other woman. Getting involved with her would mean nothing but trouble.

Then, right before they entered the Kubek residence, Annie reached across and *patted his hand.* For a moment, the black mesh on the screen door went red. Nobody, especially nobody who could kiss like Annie Kubek, was going to dismiss him with a sisterly pat on the hand.

His vision cleared as he followed Annie into the house, and he spotted his mother, her plaster-encased leg resting on an ottoman, in the cozy living room with Mrs. Kubek. Their heads were bent together as though they'd been deep in conversation. They looked up, and twin smiles wreathed their faces. Michael forced his lips to respond.

"Did you two have a nice walk?" his mother asked.

"Very nice," Annie answered, as though everything was settled between them. He took a step closer to Annie and enjoyed the puzzled look she shot him.

"Did you ask him?" Mrs. Kubek asked, distracting her so she looked at her mother instead of moving away from him.

"Mom," Annie said, and it sounded like a warning.

"Ask me what?"

"If you'd take her to her cousin Walter's wedding,"

Mrs. Kubek answered, and Annie rolled her eyes. "The people in our family, they're, well, uh, interested in the other people in our family. If Annie shows up without a date, she'll be answering questions the whole night about why she doesn't have a man with her."

"I'm sure Michael has better things to do than—"

"I'd be happy to accompany Annie," Michael interrupted, feeling as though a little devil were sitting on his shoulder spurring him on. He wondered if the little devil was as inexplicably attracted to Annie as he was. "We wouldn't want anyone to drive Annie crazy, now would we?"

He was rewarded with identical smiles from his mother and Mrs. Kubek. From Annie, he got a glower ferocious enough to fell an attacking beast.

He smiled back as though he didn't notice her displeasure, then reached across the space separating them and patted her hand.

Chapter Three

"Well, how do you think he likes Annie?" Rose Kubek whispered the next afternoon as she and Christine stood at the front door of her cozy house waving good-bye to Michael.

"Why are we whispering?" Christine whispered back as Michael got into her sturdy four-door Volvo and drove off. "Is Annie here?"

"Nobody's here but us."

"Thank goodness." Christine dropped her crutches and bent at the waist to fiddle with her cast. She gave a few deft pulls and a couple of wriggles. The plaster parted like the Red Sea and clanked to the floor.

"What are you doing?" Rose all but shrieked.

"What does it look like I'm doing? I'm freeing myself of my burden." Christine bent down and scratched

37

the skin that had been covered in plaster. "I itch more than Lady Godiva in poison ivy."

"But you can't take off the cast! What if somebody comes home unexpectedly and sees? They'll know your leg isn't really broken."

Christine picked up the plaster and made her way to the sofa. She sat down and resumed scratching. "That's why you're going to keep a lookout. It's the least you can do after you talked me into this. You can't imagine how guilty I feel lying to my son."

"How else were we going to get him to Elmwood?" Rose asked as she settled herself into a chair with a view of the street. "You said yourself he wouldn't take time off work unless you did something drastic."

"I still wish I hadn't lied about breaking my leg. He wants to hire somebody to help me get around before he goes back to California. And you should hear the lectures he's given me on cleaning up after myself and watching where I'm going."

"That's because you said you slipped on a banana peel! What was with that? Had you just finished watching the Road Runner on TV or what? Did the little critter pull one over on Wile E. Coyote?"

Christine's mouth turned down. "Michael asked how I'd broken my leg. What was I supposed to say?"

"How about your parachute wouldn't open on your sky jump? Or you took a tumble down a ski slope? Or you took a shortcut across a soccer game in progress and got kicked in the shin?"

"You're obviously a better liar than I am."

"Why, thank you, Christine," Rose said, beaming. The telephone rang, and she reached over and picked up the extension on the side table next to her chair. She listened gravely for a few moments, nodding, before covering the receiver and gazing across the room at her friend.

"It's Annie calling to say something's wrong with your phone," she said in a stage whisper. "We were right. She's been trying to get in touch with Michael, but every time she calls there's a click and then a hang-up."

"That's what you told me to do when I saw one of her numbers come up on caller ID."

"She says she's not getting anything at all right now except a busy signal."

"I took the phone off the hook before I had Michael drive me over here," Christine said.

Rose gave her a thumbs-up, uncovered the receiver, and spoke into it in a normal voice. "No, honey, I haven't had any trouble getting through to her house. What did you want to talk to him about? Maybe I could get Christine to give him a message."

After more head bobbing and another few moments, Rose hung up. "Annie wouldn't say why she was calling your house, but we were right to take precautions. I just know she's trying to get out of that date with Michael."

Christine frowned. "But I thought you said she'd fallen for him."

"She *has* fallen for him. She just doesn't know it yet." Rose tapped her chin. "What about Michael? How do you think he liked Annie?"

Christine bit her upper lip. "I don't know, Rosie. I asked him that on the way back to my place last night.

He just gave me an odd look and laughed. Maybe this isn't going to work."

"Nonsense," Rose said, shaking her head. "It's going to work just fine. They're going to the wedding together, aren't they?"

There was absolutely no way she was going to a wedding with Michael Reeves.

Even if she died between now and tomorrow and somebody tried to drag her there, Annie would muster the will to resurrect and walk stiffly in the opposite direction.

Annie frowned, because at the moment she was walking toward Michael instead of away from him. The only scenario any worse would be if Lou Spinelli opened the door to Michael's mother's house and threatened her again. For an awful moment, the park manager's face swam before her eyes as she remembered what he'd told her just an hour ago.

"All it would take to get those birds taken away from you is one word from me." Spinelli had advanced so close she could smell the cloying scent of the wintergreen gum he always chewed, but she'd refused to back away. "Think about that, Annie. Think about that."

Her heart constricted at the thought of losing the majestic hawks, falcons, owls, and vultures that made their home at the park. Since all of them were injured too severely to survive in the wild, where else would they go?

Determinedly, she shook off the specter of the park

manager. Saving her raptors was tomorrow's problem. Today's was a doozy, and she had yet to tackle it.

The sidewalk led to a simple, one-story brick house surrounded by the blooms of spring. The fiery red of the azalea bushes contrasted with the white blooms of the dogwoods and pinks of the cherry trees to create a springtime treasure. The lawn had been recently mowed, and the smell of freshly cut grass mingled with the scents of the blossoms.

Christine Reeves's house was very much like Annie's. Perfect in its simplicity. Annie doubted Michael would view it that way. He belonged in an elegant dwelling in a cosmopolitan setting with bright lights shining down on him. Not in a rural community like Elmwood.

She made herself put one foot in front of the other, cursing Christine Reeves's telephone for going haywire. Breaking a date over the telephone was vastly preferable to doing it in person. Her step faltered, but she pressed on. Mrs. Reeves would undoubtedly answer the door. Annie would make small talk, ask if she could speak to Michael, break the date, and leave. What could possibly be easier?

She pressed her forefinger to the doorbell, affixing a smile for Mrs. Reeves. The door swung open, but it was Michael who answered it.

Despite his casual clothes and tousled hair, he looked only slightly less perfect than he had the night before. His jeans weren't new, but they were casually chic and probably stonewashed instead of faded. His T-shirt was so unwrinkled she wouldn't have been surprised if he'd ironed it, his athletic shoes so white they had to be new.

She took in his too-green eyes, too-straight nose, too-high cheekbones, and the way his mouth curved into a smile at the sight of her. She touched her lips, involuntarily remembering how heavenly that mouth felt against hers. His eyes followed the motion, and his smile widened. Annie jerked her hand downward, horrified by what she might have revealed.

Although it had taken every morsel of her will-power, she had successfully convinced him a kiss as unsettling as an earthquake had been merely adequate. She couldn't have him guessing the truth, especially because her inexplicable reaction to him didn't change a thing.

She still wasn't going to marry him. Or, for that matter, take him to Walter's wedding.

"Don't tell me you've decided I'm your type after all?" he asked, his brow wrinkling in amusement. For a moment, she thought he'd known she was thinking of his kiss. Then she realized he was referring to her presence at his mother's home.

"That's not funny," she said and took a step back-ward. There wasn't any need to test what his proximity would do to her equilibrium. She already knew. "I came here to tell you I don't need you to go with me to Walter's wedding."

His eyes narrowed, and his smile disappeared. She had the uncomfortable feeling he was looking into her soul. "That's not the only thing on your mind, is it? Something else is wrong. Believe it or not, I can be an awfully good listener."

"Nothing else is wrong," Annie said automatically, but she was shaken by his insight. For a fleeting moment, she wanted to confide in him about Lou Spinelli and the threat to her raptors. But that was ridiculous. She could handle her own problems. "The only thing on my mind is Walter's wedding."

His smile again firmly in place, he gestured toward the inside of the house. "If that's your story," he said, managing to convey that he didn't entirely believe her, "why don't you come inside so we can talk about Walter's wedding?"

She had the sudden, absurd notion that it would be dangerous to accept his invitation and enter his world. That, once she did, she wouldn't be able to turn back. She planted her feet firmly on the sidewalk as she gazed at him.

"There's nothing to talk about." The setting sun backlit his hair, making it resemble the color of freshly cut wheat, and she tried to remember what she had thought was wrong with it. She squinted, shutting out the sun and the image. "I said what I had to say. Now I'm leaving."

"You're not playing fair, Annie." He shook his head, as though disappointed in her. "I haven't said what I have to say yet."

"What could you possibly have to say?"

"How about this? I'm not such a bad guy that you should treat me like an enemy just because your mother wants you to treat me like a friend."

"A friend?" Annie blurted the word. "That's understating the case. She wants me to treat you like a fiancé. Like, like . . . the man of my dreams!"

"I'd appreciate it," he said, blowing out a breath that ruffled the hair above his brow, "if you wouldn't treat me like the man of your nightmares. Now are you going to come in so we can discuss this like rational adults?"

"There's nothing rational about our situation," Annie muttered, but she moved toward him just the same. His mother was in the house, after all. It wasn't like she'd be alone with him.

Before she could pass, he snagged her hand and smiled as though it were perfectly natural for them to enter his mother's house hand in hand. His was warm and dry and . . . exciting.

"The cleaning lady I hired just left. She waxed the wood floor, and I wouldn't want you to trip," he said as he led her into his house, but her heart was already tripping. She took a deep breath to steady herself . . . and caught his scent.

He smelled as good as he had the night before, like soap and shampoo and an intoxicating something that could only have been man. Funny. She would have thought he'd be the kind of man to drench himself in cologne. He probably kept forgetting to put it on.

He slowed his steps unexpectedly, and her momentum brought her so close to him that for a moment she couldn't breathe. She felt his breath rustle the hair at her temples, sending a warm shiver down the length of her body. Her eyes were at the level of his mouth, and she suddenly remembered she hadn't found anything objectionable about it. Not in the luscious way his lips curved around his teeth when he smiled. Nor in the delicious way his mouth tasted when it was molded to hers.

Calling herself all kinds of a fool, she tugged her hand from his and sidestepped. She staggered, and righted herself with a steadying hand against a wall. When she was clear of him, she could breathe again.

"I was just about to break for dinner," Michael said, indicating the laptop computer and papers strewn over the kitchen table. He looked completely unaffected by her presence. That irritated her almost as much as her reaction to him. "Why don't I throw on an extra burger for you?"

"Burgers?" she asked dumbly. "You eat burgers?"

"Why wouldn't I eat burgers?" A puzzled frown creased his brow. She could have kicked herself. Any tact she possessed, which admittedly wasn't much, obviously went on hiatus whenever she got anywhere near Michael. As did her common sense.

"Just because I didn't grow up in the United States doesn't mean I'm not American. I like hot dogs and apple pie, too." He grinned at her. "Not to mention the girl next door."

"I was never the girl next door," Annie retorted, her gaze sliding away from his as she felt heat rise to her face. She was at a complete loss as to why she was letting him unsettle her. Everybody knew Annie Kubek didn't get flustered. Especially not by citified men who weren't her type.

"Nope. You were just a young, pretty thing who lived in the neighborhood and liked to go topless."

"I was a baby! It's not like I was wearing a bikini bottom, for Pete's sake. It was a diaper!"

All Annie's outburst got her was a laugh from Michael and an admonition from herself to stop letting him unsettle her.

"Somewhere, in the recesses of my memory," he said when he'd stopped laughing, "I seem to remember you looked awfully good in a diaper."

Instead of answering, she scowled and looked around for Mrs. Reeves. After a few moments, she realized that not only couldn't she see her, but she couldn't hear her either.

"Where's your mother?"

"Your mother invited her to dinner. I had some work to do, so I said I'd fend for myself."

Funny that her mother hadn't mentioned Mrs. Reeves was visiting when she'd called an hour ago, Annie thought. Her suspicious eyes scanned the room, settling on the phone. Its receiver was askew, which Annie couldn't quite believe was due to carelessness. Had their mothers anticipated that she'd try to break the date and arranged it so she'd have to do so in person?

"What do you say to that burger?" Michael asked, and it occurred to Annie that she was alone in the house with him. Alone. Where they were perfectly free to replicate the kissing experiment from yesterday.

"No! I mean, no thanks. I'm not staying long," Annie said, biting her lip as she fought her nerves. She leaned against the wall, increasing the distance between them.

"Let me ask you something," Michael asked, and she braced herself for another question about kisses.

"Do you know anyone around here looking to make some easy money?"

The question was so unexpected that she just stared at him.

"I want to hire somebody to help my mom out after I leave town," he said, smiling at her. "Call me an overprotective son, but I'm the only family she has left. When my father died a few years ago, I promised myself I'd look out for her. That's hard to do now that she's in Elmwood, but I want to make sure she's okay before I leave."

Something softened inside Annie at his explanation, and she remembered his plea not to treat him like the enemy. He wasn't that, not by a long shot, but she wasn't about to let herself get too involved with him. Her mother's insistent pushing aside, he lived in a different world than she did. One with cities and traffic and stress.

"I could give you a couple of names," she said. "When are you looking to hire someone?"

"As soon as possible," Michael said. Then, unexpectedly, his eyes twinkled. "Because of my too-ambitious tendencies, I can't afford to be away from CompTech's corporate headquarters for more than a few weeks."

"Because you're so set on making this vice presidency?"

"Because I *am* going to make vice president," Michael countered. "I know you don't find working hard to be particularly admirable, but that's what us too-ambitious guys do. Other employees might be content to stay at the bottom of the ladder, but we climb it rung by rung to the top."

"What's at the top that's so all-fired important?"

His mouth opened, but he didn't answer immediately. "Why, uh . . . success," he said finally. "That's what."

Annie thought that was a poor response, but she wasn't in the mood to get into a discussion about the pitfalls of too much ambition. Even if she were right. Take Lucifer, for example. He'd had too much ambition, and look where he'd ended up: the pits of the Inferno. "So, to get this success, you have to live in Los Angeles."

"There's something to say for showing your face day after day in the office where the decision makers are."

"Are you sure you're going to be able to survive two weeks away from the spotlight?" Annie asked. "There aren't any nightclubs or health spas or fine dining in Elmwood. The nearest movie theater is thirty miles away and doesn't show first-run films."

"You're forgetting that my roots are here, Annie. My mother loves Elmwood. Maybe I will, too."

"I hear your father couldn't wait to leave."

"My father could never have reached the rank of general in the Air Force if he'd stayed here. He taught me that success isn't something that comes to you. You have to chase it."

"There isn't anything to chase in Elmwood."

"I don't know about that." He let his eyes rest on her. If she hadn't known better, she would have thought he was flirting with her. "Maybe I'll have a better handle on the town after your cousin's wedding."

"But you're not going to Walter's wedding," she protested.

"It doesn't seem that way at the moment," he said easily and smiled at her. "But I will be once I talk you out of uninviting me."

His smile, Annie was sure, wasn't one of the things she'd told him she disliked. True, his teeth were a bit too straight. But his lips were full and luscious, rendering his smile just shy of devastating and driving home the unwelcome thought that she had developed a fixation on his mouth.

"I didn't invite you to the wedding in the first place." Annie dragged her eyes from his mouth. Belatedly, the meaning of his claim occurred to her. "And you're not going to be able to talk me out of anything."

"That's yet to be seen." Michael glanced at her before walking to the refrigerator, tall, loose-limbed, and impossibly riveting. "Have a seat at the kitchen table, and I'll pour you a glass of lemonade."

"There's no point in talking about this," Annie said, but she pulled out one of the slat-backed wooden chairs and sat.

"Sure, there is," Michael said, carrying two glasses to the table. He placed one in front of her before seating himself at an angle to her.

He took a long drink of lemonade, and she found herself watching his Adam's apple bob as he swallowed. He licked some lemonade off his lips, and she forced herself to look away. She focused on a spot somewhere beyond his left shoulder.

He turned and looked behind him. "Do you see something back there?"

"No," she said, feeling foolish.

"Are you sure? I thought you were looking at something behind me."

"I'm not," Annie mumbled. He returned his attention to her, and she didn't have any choice but to look him in the eyes. Too green. She'd told him they were too green. And they were. Ridiculously green. Like the leaves of the trees that shaded Elmwood in the summer. Whoever heard of a man having eyes as green as that?

"Since we've established that you don't see anything over my shoulder," he said, "let's talk about my mouth."

"Your mouth?" Annie's eyes immediately dropped to his mouth, at which she had been trying valiantly not to stare. Why did he want to talk about that delectable mouth? She cleared her throat. "I'm afraid I don't follow."

The mouth smiled, slow and wide. A pulse leaped in her throat. She wondered if he were going to bring up The Kiss. She wondered what she would say if he did. She hoped she wouldn't suggest they try it again.

"I don't go back on the words that come out of it," he said instead, "and I said I'd go with you to Walter's wedding. So I'll go with you."

Her gaze shot to his eyes. "But I just said I don't need you to!"

He perched his elbows on the table and leaned toward her. She looked away, picked up her lemonade, and drank deeply, using the glass to shield at least part of her from his perusal. Eventually, she had to put the glass down. Eventually, she had to meet those ridiculously green eyes again.

"What about all those relatives who'll give you a hard time about showing up without a date?"

"I've just about got them convinced I'm not the marrying kind, so I figure I can handle them." Annie shifted in her seat. Although it was a cool spring day, she thought his kitchen was much too warm. "It's better than having to explain why I'm there with you."

"Why can't you just tell the truth?"

Her eyes grew as round as the burgers he wanted to cook for them. "You want me to tell them our mothers are so certain we're destined to be together that they betrothed us in infancy?"

"No, of course not," he said, but his grin made another appearance. The power of it knocked her back a few inches and she fought to keep from swaying. "I meant you should say I'm a family friend who's visiting and looking forward to meeting some of the townspeople."

"You are?" she asked, the words twin syllables of surprise. "Are you trying to say you *want* to go to the wedding?"

"That's exactly what I'm saying." His smile faded. "Why is that so hard to believe?"

She bit her lip, considering whether he was telling the truth. It occurred to her that it was quite possible he thought he was being truthful. After all, he had no

way of knowing what attending a wedding in Elmwood entailed.

"It's hard to believe somebody like you would enjoy
himself at a wedding like this one's going to be," she
said finally, being as tactful as she knew how to be.

He cocked an eyebrow. "Oh, and why wouldn't
someone like me enjoy a wedding in Elmwood?"

"Because . . ." Annie grasped for the right words to
explain. She couldn't find them, so she gave up on
tact. "Because it's going to be a big, loud Polish wedding with a polka band, lots of people, lots of food,
and lots of booze. It won't be one of those elegant
little affairs with piano music and those fancy hors
d'oeuvres you're undoubtedly used to."

He was silent for a moment, digesting that. "You're
pretty big on stereotypes, aren't you?"

"Why shouldn't I be?" She assumed a defensive
posture with her back pressed as far back against the
chair as possible. "I've usually found that what you
see is what you get."

"Does that mean you're exactly what you seem?"

Her eyes narrowed. She didn't want to ask the obvious question, but she couldn't help herself. "How do
I seem?"

"Like one of those women who don't bother with
frills and who doesn't care what anybody thinks of
her."

"Why should I care?" Annie retorted and then
frowned. "What do you mean about the frills?"

He laughed, reached across the table to pick up one
of her hands, and examined her short, blunt finger-
nails. Instead of just touching her fingers, he seemed

to stroke them. She pulled her hand away and immediately missed his warmth.

"Just as I thought. No nail polish. You're not wearing makeup either, not that you need any. But most of the women I know wouldn't leave home without makeup. They wouldn't put on that park ranger uniform, either, but you even wear it after hours."

"Why shouldn't I?" Annie asked, but she was acutely conscious that her uniform concealed her curves. Irritation bubbled at the thought that she'd even want them on display. That she would want Michael Reeves to think of her as desirable. "Clothes are just packaging. What matters is what's underneath."

"Still," he said consideringly, "I'm looking forward to this wedding tomorrow. You're so covered up all the time you've got me wondering whether you've actually got legs under those trousers. I'm hoping you won't wear that uniform to the wedding."

"So we're back to the wedding," Annie said, ignoring his last comment. Michael was an intelligent man, one who couldn't have missed the way he'd made her blush. She suspected he was deliberately trying to disconcert her now, and she couldn't have him think he was succeeding.

"Yes, we're back to the wedding. Despite what you said about the noise and the food and the booze, I still want to go." He reached across the table and touched her cheek. "What do you say, Annie? Can I go to the wedding with you? Please?"

Annie's resolve, so strong when she'd entered his house, weakened like a limp French fry. She leaned back imperceptibly, and his hand fell from her face.

She'd be able to think more clearly, she thought crossly, if he'd only stop touching her.

"Don't you realize the problems that would create? Our mothers will think this pact thing is working!"

"Annie." He reached across the table and took her hand. This time his touch made the little hairs on her arm stand at attention. "If there is a pact, we're going to have to deal with it sooner or later."

"What do you mean *if* there is a pact?" Annie asked, wondering whether he was one of those touchy-feely people who was always grabbing others. While she was wondering, she let her hand remain in his. "Didn't you ask your mother about it?"

"I didn't want to put her on the spot," he said slowly. "She obviously likes you, and I'm sure she'd be pleased if we fell in love. But I'm just not convinced she's in on a pact."

That did it. She pulled her hand away from his. Again.

"Not in on it? Of course she's in on it. The phone's off the hook, for goodness sake. And what do you mean if we fall in love? I'm telling you, they think we've been in love for almost twenty-five years. They think we're destined to be together!"

He gave her a calm, level look, which made her feel like a raving madwoman.

"Annie, I'm going to be in Elmwood for two weeks. Since our mothers are best friends, it stands to reason we'll run into each other. Wouldn't it be better if we formed a pact of our own?"

"What kind of pact?" Annie asked suspiciously.

"The kind of pact where we decide to get along,"

he said. "The kind of pact where you don't wave what your mother thinks in front of my face every time we're together."

Annie thought for a minute, wondering how childish she would seem if she refused. Exceedingly childish, she concluded. Besides, why shouldn't she agree? It wasn't as though he were her type.

"I guess I can do that," she said, rising to her feet and starting to back out of the kitchen. "As long as you realize you're not my type."

"You've already made that perfectly clear." He frowned, got out of his chair, and followed her. "So we're on for the wedding, right? Just tell me what time to pick you up."

"Four o'clock," she said, bumping into a wall in her haste to make a retreat. She blabbed the first thing that came to mind to cover her stumble. "The church service starts at four-thirty, and it probably won't be over until five-thirty. Don't say I didn't warn you. This won't be one of those short, sweet, impersonal services people in the city have."

"People in the city go to church, Annie. I've actually been there myself," Michael said, still following her. He frowned. "You don't have to go yet, you know."

"Oh, yes I do," she answered before she escaped out the front door and into the sweet, fresh air. She wrinkled her nose at her mental use of the word escape.

Just what she had escaped, she couldn't say. But then she couldn't say why she was going with him to Walter's wedding, either.

Chapter Four

Michael pulled the note off Annie's front door and crumpled it, shaking his head. Annie had seriously underestimated him if she thought she could dodge his company by scrawling a few cryptic sentences.

Emergency at the park, she'd written. *Go ahead without me.*

He should have expected her to avoid him after the skittish way she'd acted yesterday, but the bald truth was that he hadn't. Instead, he'd been congratulating himself for getting her to keep the date and wondering what she'd look like in a dress.

He could go to the wedding without her. The rest of the Kubeks, as well as his mother, were going to be there. But if he went alone, Annie would take it as an excuse to treat him like any one of a hundred other guests rather than as her date.

And, darn it, that would be as bad as letting her get away with patting his hand after kissing him.

Not only was she going to kiss him again and like it, but she was going to the wedding with him even if he had to go to the park and fetch her.

Ten minutes later, he stood inside the building that housed the headquarters of the Green Forest Nature Center.

"Can I help you?" A middle-aged blond with twin dimples, dressed in the drab green ranger get-up Annie wore, looked up from the group of children surrounding her. At first glance, she seemed to be holding a thick, black ribbon. Michael took a few steps closer to the group, then a few steps back. The ribbon was alive. "Dressed like that, I doubt you're here to learn about black rat snakes."

"Good guess." He glanced down at his slate-gray Armani suit. "I'm sorry to interrupt, but can you tell me where to find Annie Kubek?"

"You're looking for Annie, are you?" The woman chuckled. But it wasn't the kind of laughter that Annie had broken into when she'd first seen him. There was something commiserating about this woman's laughter. He was pretty sure that wasn't a good thing.

She disentangled herself from the group and walked to his side, still holding the snake. With residents like that, the nature center didn't need a security system.

"She's outside with Mr. Hoots," the woman said

low enough that only he could hear. "Just walk through the back door and head for the woods."

Michael smiled and thanked her, but scowled as he went in search of Annie. So she was with Mr. Hoots, was she? He ran a hand through his hair, remembering Annie had said it was too short and stylish when relaying the reasons he wasn't her type.

He wondered if this Mr. Hoots was her type. He was probably dark-haired, dark-eyed, and, in keeping with her aversion to "too-tall" men like himself, short. Michael already disliked him.

He followed the dirt path that cut a trail behind the building and stopped when he rounded the first bend. A connected series of wood and wire cages, about fifteen feet high and so artfully constructed they seemed to be part of the woods, backed up to the thick underbrush. From inside one of the cages, he heard a familiar voice speaking with unfamiliar gentleness.

"Stop trying to get away from me, Hoots." The slight breeze rustling his hair carried Annie's voice. "You know I'm your friend. Your best girl. I love you to death. Don't look at me so doubtfully with those big, dark eyes. I'm telling the truth. I love you, big guy. You're the only one for me."

So that was it, Michael thought with a burst of hot, raw disappointment. Annie wasn't interested in him because she was in love with this Hoots character. Just what did this guy have that he didn't, anyway?

He ate up the ground leading to the cage with long, frenzied strides. Annie was standing with her back toward him in the middle of a cage that counted a fallen log and leafy branches as decor. Incredibly, she was alone.

His eyes darted around the cage, searching for the mysterious Lothario she called Mr. Hoots, but no other man was in sight. Then he heard flapping and a distinctive, "Hoot. Hoot." His gaze was drawn downward to the corner of the cage.

Mr. Hoots certainly was short. He probably didn't even top two feet.

He was also an owl.

"Stop that flapping, Hoots," Annie continued in the same soothing tone. "It's okay now. Annie's here. Yes, she is."

Michael hung his head, feeling foolish. She was talking to an owl, for goodness sake. She murmured some nonsense words in the soft voice that was as warm as the wind, and he couldn't help wishing she'd speak to him that way.

She wasn't wearing a dress, but a pantsuit with a short, stylish jacket so white it contrasted vividly with her dark hair. High heels made legs covered by slim black slacks appear miles long. His gaze followed the length of those legs upward, thinking it was a crime that she wore her uniform trousers so baggy.

"Calm down, good-looking. Annie loves you. Yes, she does." She took a step closer to the owl. Mr. Hoots stopped flapping and gazed at her through his round eyes. Adoringly, Michael thought. What male wouldn't respond that way when she turned sugar-sweet on him? Mr. Hoots was one lucky owl.

Oh, great. Now he was letting himself become envious of an owl.

The owl's eyes fastened on him at the same moment the woman's did. If anything, the owl looked more welcoming.

"I thought I told you to go ahead without me," Annie said, no longer using the velvety voice that warmed his insides.

"What? And deny myself the pleasure of your company?" Michael walked the rest of the way to the cage as Annie's gaze skimmed him from head to toe before coming to rest on his face.

"Do I pass?" he asked with a lift of his eyebrows.

"You'll do," she said, then smiled. It drew his attention to her mouth, which looked as though she might have run a swipe of lipstick across it. He wouldn't swear to it, but it was also possible she was wearing mascara. Not that she needed any. "That's a designer suit, isn't it? And I bet that tie cost the earth."

He glanced down at the silk tie, which had swirls of burgundy and gray running through it. "I bought it because I liked it, not because of the label on it."

"And that's why you bought the suit, too?" Her eyes twinkled as though there was something inherently funny about owning an Armani suit.

"Never mind why I bought the suit," Michael said. Part of becoming successful was dressing the part, but she wouldn't understand that. "Why aren't you wearing a dress?"

"I didn't want to tell you this before," she answered, looking straight into his eyes. "But remember when you said you were wondering whether I had legs under my trousers?" He nodded. "Well, I don't."

"Very funny," he said, and she laughed.

"Hoot, hoot." The owl that had been cowering in the corner hopped forward and stared at Michael, and he could have sworn he saw dislike in his eyes. "Hoot, hoot."

"Aren't you going to introduce us?" Michael asked, feeling as though he were cutting in on another male's date.

"Certainly." Annie turned to look at the owl. He had ears that stood at attention, a mottled brown body, and a white throat. "This beautiful boy here is Mr. Hoots. He's a great horned owl."

"Hoot, hoot," the owl called again, but to Michael it sounded like, "shoo, shoo."

"Why does he hop around like that?"

"The woman who brought him here cut into his wing so he wouldn't fly away, except now he can't fly at all. He's really very social." She looked at the owl. "Aren't you, big boy? That's why you get into trouble, did you know that?"

To Michael, she said, "Some kid poked a long stick through his cage this morning, and he went nuts. Miriam, that's the other park naturalist, couldn't settle him down. So here I am."

"So you mean that note on your door was legitimate?"

"Of course it was." Annie smiled again. "What did you think I was trying to do, duck you?"

"The thought crossed my mind."

"Mine, too," Annie confessed. "I still think going to the wedding with you, when our mothers have this pact thing hanging over us, is a very bad idea."

So she was back to the pact. If there really were

such a thing, he wondered if their mothers knew it was making Annie even more resistant to him. He frowned, remembering her reaction when she first saw him. Maybe she was predisposed to resist him.

"We've gone over this ground already," he said. "We agreed to make a pact of our own to get along."

"That was your idea, not mine." Annie put her hands on her hips and sent him a worried look. The sunlight filtered through the cage and shone down on her, casting a reddish glow that infused her with life. Despite her tousled hair and the pantsuit that covered just about every inch of her, she was the most attractive woman he'd ever seen.

"You agreed to it," he pointed out.

"In a weak moment," she said warily. "We're not even sure we can make it work."

"If you could tear yourself away from Mr. Hoots and get out of that cage, we could go to the wedding and give it a try."

"Hoot. Hoot." The owl hopped closer to Annie and she crouched down beside him.

"I'll check on you tomorrow, love," she said, automatically softening her voice and sending another surge of envy through Michael. Before the night was over, Michael vowed, she was going to speak to him in that same satiny voice. He'd make her see that he was more her type than some midget of an owl.

"Keeeeer . . . keeeeer."

Without another word, she straightened and let herself out of the owl's cage. Michael followed her until she came to a stop in front of another cage. Perched atop a fallen tree branch was a large bird with a reddish tail and a dark bar across its belly. Nothing seemed to be amiss inside the cage, and Michael watched the tension seep out of Annie's shoulders.

"That's a falcon, right?" he asked.

"Nice try, city boy." She gave him a sidelong glance. "Tommy's a red-tailed hawk. See those two raptors in the cage next to Tommy?"

"Raptors?"

"It's another name for birds of prey. Those two are American kestrels, a kind of falcon common around these parts. Their wings are longer and bent back at an angle, unlike Tommy's. See, his wings are more rounded."

"Tommy the hawk. Tomahawk," Michael said. "Cute."

"Over here are Dr. and Mrs. Death." She walked to yet another cage. It contained two large black birds with small, unfeathered heads. "Like all our raptors, these two have permanent injuries. A drawback to being a vulture is that speeding cars rush over their dinner table. Besides having to snack on dead things, of course."

In Annie's enthusiasm to share her passion for the birds, she seemed to have forgotten to be wary of him. Her eyes shone, her expression lightened, and Michael thought he was getting a glimpse of the real Annie. "Do you have an eagle?" he asked, wanting to keep her talking.

"Injured eagles are usually put into a captive breeding program, and I don't have the facilities for that here." A wistful look crossed her face. "I'll tell you what I'd really like, though. A larger falcon, like a peregrine."

"Then why don't you get one?"

Annie harrumphed, and displeasure was evident on her expressive face. She'd make a terrible poker player, Michael thought. "Did I ask the wrong question?"

"Oh, no. It's just that I've been trying to get one here for years. Now we finally have a lead on one and some uninformed greenhorn is keeping him from us."

"Say that again in English."

"Oh, sorry." Annie sent him an apologetic glance. "We get most of our birds from a raptor rehab center. In the past, if the raptors couldn't be returned to the wild, they were offered to us. That is, until Felicity Pomposity came on the scene."

"Felicity Pomposity?"

"She goes by Felicity McMann, but my name fits her better." Annie kicked at the dirt with the toe of her shoe. "She feels it's wrong for raptors to be in cages. She doesn't understand that, because of their shrinking habitat, man is the greatest enemy these birds face. She doesn't grasp how important it is to educate the public about them."

"If they can't survive in the wild," Michael asked, perplexed, "what does she think should be done to them?"

"She'd rather euthanize them than give them to me," Annie said acridly. She took a deep breath, seeming to make a supreme effort to collect herself. "But that's a problem for another day. We might as well get this wedding over with. We're already late."

"We're going to be even later after you stop home to change your clothes."

Annie's reaction was immediate. She put her hands on her hips and glared up at him in one of the best shows of independence he'd ever seen. He thought she looked magnificent.

"Listen, Buster, I'm not about to go home and change my clothes because you have some hankering to see my legs. I don't know where you get off—"

"Annie."

"—thinking that you can tell me—"

"Annie."

"*What?*" she shouted at him in all-too-obvious exasperation.

"Take a look at the right side of your jacket."

She looked, and her jaw-dropping expression was priceless. A greenish-brown smear extended a good four inches above the hemline of her white jacket down to the hip of her black slacks.

"Oh, great," Annie muttered.

Michael suppressed a smile and silently chalked one up for the birds.

Chapter Five

Even though she was sitting down, with her legs tucked under a round table that seated eight, Annie tugged the skirt of her dress toward her knees. It fell short by a good six inches, making her curse the day she'd let her sister Ruth talk her into buying it.

It should have been enough that she'd worn a flouncy, floor-length bridesmaid gown in petal-pink when Ruth had married. She shouldn't have had to honor the bride's request that she wear a dress to the rehearsal and dinner.

She certainly shouldn't have let Ruth bully her into choosing this dress, she thought as she rubbed her hands over her bare arms. It had a lace outerlay in a swirling, intricate pattern atop a nylon shell that was nearly the color of her flesh. Suddenly uncomfortable,

Annie grabbed a piece of the nylon and pulled it away from her skin, but when she let it go it sprung back in place.

She gave another ineffectual tug at her hemline and blushed when she thought of the way Michael's eyes had lingered on her legs. Ruth picked that moment to smile at Annie from across the table. Annie scowled back, conveniently disregarding the fact that she wouldn't have had anything else suitable to wear if Ruth hadn't talked her into buying The Dress. Her sodden pantsuit represented her only other wedding-appropriate clothing.

"The Dress looks very nice," Ruth said. At her side, the husband for whom she'd sacrificed Elmwood nodded. He was a nice guy, but he was from Chicago. Annie thought Ruth should have held out for a man who would have moved his life to Elmwood instead of expecting her to uproot hers to Chicago.

"He must be very special, this fiancé of yours, for you to be wearing The Dress," her Aunt Eugenia said, and Annie thanked the stars that Michael was off at the moment getting them drinks. Aunt Eugenia smiled widely. A swipe of her primrose-pink lipstick had missed her lips and ended up on her teeth. Beside her, as was his custom, Annie's Uncle Janos said nothing. "So are you going to tell us where you've been hiding him? He's a catch, he is. As charming as the day is long. So how come the first time I meet him is a few hours ago at the church?"

"Michael is not my fiancé," Annie said, for what seemed like the hundredth time that day. Aunt Eugenia frowned, an expression at odds with the huge yellow sunflowers that cheerfully decorated her floor-length dress. Her lipstick-smeared teeth bit into her bottom lip. Uncle Janos stared.

"I was sure your mother said he was."

"Well, he's not," Annie snapped, and then immediately felt ashamed. Aunt Eugenia and Uncle Janos, who were childless, had lived within a baseball throw of her parents for as long as Annie remembered. Snapping at her aunt because she was interested in what was happening in Annie's life was not only senseless, but mean-spirited.

"I'm sorry, Aunt Eugenia." Annie suppressed a sigh. "I didn't mean to snap at you, but we're not engaged."

The older woman clucked her lips and patted Annie's hand. "I can understand why you're upset about it, Annie dear, with him being so handsome and all. But I'm sure you can steer him to the altar if you work on it."

All around the table, various cousins and other relations nodded sympathetically.

Annie gnawed the inside of her cheek so she wouldn't scream in frustration. Michael was approaching from behind, so she raised her voice. Hopefully, he'd size up the situation and come to her rescue. "There is nothing romantic going on between me and Michael."

"Hey, there, beautiful."

The words went through her brain like a shock wave, but before she could angrily brand him as a traitor he added another tremor by nuzzling his delectable lips against her neck. It unsettled her so much that goose bumps danced on her flesh. Aunt Eugenia flashed her a satisfied grin.

"I see I made it back before dinner was served." Michael smiled at everyone at the table as though he'd known them for years. "I wasn't sure what you wanted, Annie, so I took a guess and brought you a ginger ale."

Annie wouldn't have admitted it was her favorite soft drink even if an afternoon of white-water rafting was at stake. She took the drink he offered with fingers that shook and berated herself for the shaking.

"Thank you," she said, and even her voice quivered. Darn the infernal, aggravating man. He wasn't at all her type, but there was something about him that discombobulated her. He casually draped his free arm around her shoulder, and she gritted her teeth.

"If you don't get your arm off me in the next five seconds," she whispered so he alone could hear, "I'm going to have to hurt you."

Although he honored her request, to her consternation he did it with a grin and a tap on her nose. "That's what I like about you, Annie," he said, running his eyes over her face in a way the others at the table probably perceived as romantic. "You have such a charming way with words."

Then he reached for his glass and took a long pull of . . . beer? Annie narrowed her unbelieving eyes.

"Is that beer you're drinking?"

"The last time I looked, it was," he said and then grimaced with a theatrical flair. He lowered his voice. "Don't tell me beer-drinking is another thing you dislike in a man."

"No. I like men who drink beer just fine," she whispered back. "I just didn't expect you to be one of them."

"Why's that?"

Because you're so urbane, Annie thought. *Because beer is the working man's drink of choice, the kind that goes down nice and easy during a night at the neighborhood pool hall.* She was sure he wouldn't know a pool cue from a curlicue.

"You just look like your tastes would run more to aged cabernet sauvignon or a glass of port than beer," she said aloud.

"Hasn't anyone ever told you that appearances can be deceiving?" he asked, and she stopped her lips from curling in amusement. But just barely. In her experience, she usually found that what she saw was what she got.

Lucia Novak, whose three daughters had been contemporaries of Annie's before they'd married and had children, beamed a smile so wide it looked like her too-heavy makeup was cracking.

"I think it's so cute the way the two of you are whispering sweet nothings to each other," she announced loudly. Her husband was sitting beside her, and she elbowed him so hard that half the contents of his drink drenched the table. "Isn't it lovely that Annie has found herself a man? I knew it was serious as soon as I saw her in The Dress. According to Rose, it won't be long before we have another wedding to go to."

"Oh, for goodness sake," Annie muttered under her breath. Just a moment ago, she'd been congratulating herself for having avoided sitting with either her mother or Mrs. Reeves, but she'd landed at an even more nightmarish table.

She was preparing to issue another denial when an army of waitresses interrupted her by descending on their table with steaming plates of stuffed cabbage rolls, pierogi, and kielbasa. Although she knew the food must be foreign to him, Michael dug into it with relish and easily slipped into the ebb and flow of conversation around the table.

She frowned at him while he ate and talked and charmed. His arm was no longer around her, but she was so conscious of him it could have been. Just then he gave her a smile that seemed to say he knew that. She glared back. Drat the man.

A metallic clanging started across the hall, and all around them the wedding guests picked up their silverware and banged it against their plates. Annie lifted her fork to join in the ruckus, but Michael appeared stupefied. He leaned nearer to her, and she breathed in the now-familiar mix of soap, shampoo, and the scintillating something that was distinctly Michael.

"What's everyone doing?"

"Banging on their plates," she said. He looked so puzzled that she forgot she was annoyed with him and grinned. "It's a Polish custom. You're supposed to kiss when the guests do that."

Michael's impossibly green eyes widened, then darkened. Inexplicably, he shrugged. "Okay," he said.

In the next instant, Michael's lips captured hers. It happened so swiftly that Annie was dizzy with the speed of it. At least that's what she told herself as he easily rendered her as mindless as he had the first time he kissed her.

She dropped her fork, threaded her hands through his hair, and kissed him back on his beautiful mouth. He tasted faintly of beer, but more intoxicating, and she wanted the kiss never to end. But then, incredibly, he drew back.

"I like that custom." He stared into her eyes and whispered so only she could hear. "But we shouldn't do too much of that in public."

In public? Annie blinked so hard that her predicament became as clear as spun glass. They'd just been kissing in public! What's more, the public consisted of a crowd of her relatives and friends who thought she and Michael were headed for the altar. She disentangled her fingers from his hair and thumped him on the arm. Hard.

"I didn't mean you were supposed to kiss me," she chastised, looking at him in horror. "When you bang the silverware, the *bride and groom* are supposed to kiss for luck. Not the guests."

"Sorry," Michael said, but his smile told her he was anything but. Worse, the other six people at the table were looking at them with what Annie recognized as approval.

Aunt Eugenia even clapped.

The strands of a polka band filled the hall, sending gaily dressed revelers bolting for the dance floor, where they whirled and twirled to the beat. Annie stood at the edge of the crowd, annoyed that Michael had so aggravated her that she couldn't even tap her toes in time with the music.

Cousin Walter had wed a Polish girl with a family that was doing its ancestors proud by hosting a wedding bash that had liquor flowing, abundant food, and gay tunes that flooded the dance floor with people.

She'd sent Michael off in search of a drink she didn't want, expressly to give herself time to recover her common sense. How the devil was she going to keep on convincing him he was all wrong for her when she kept responding to his kisses?

Worse, how was she going to convince her mother? She lifted her eyes to the ceiling, saw that it was streamed with good-luck banners, and whispered a silent prayer. *Please, please don't let my mother find out about that last kiss.* No sooner had Annie uttered the prayer than she heard her mother's voice.

"I'm not one to say I told you so," she said loudly, disregarding the fact that she most definitely was, "but I told you so. You and Michael were born for each other. But, Annie, don't you think it's a little much to be kissing him in public?"

Annie's heart sank to her naked knees. "Who told you?"

"Aunt Eugenia told Uncle Frank, who told Aunt Marta. Aunt Marta told me. They all wanted to know when the wedding was. I told them I needed at least three months of planning, so I thought we'd shoot for the first weekend in August."

Annie groaned. "Just because I kissed the man doesn't mean I'm marrying him."

Her mother's beaming smile grew so expansive it

looked as though her face would split in two. "Of course, it does. Oh, look, Annie. Speak of the devil. Here he comes."

Annie reluctantly turned her head and watched Michael walk toward them. His suit fit him to perfection, she thought as he laughed at a passing comment one of her relatives made. She still thought he was too tall and too blond with features that were entirely too sculpted, but she couldn't help wondering what *his* legs looked like under *his* trousers.

Oh, great, Annie thought as Michael's delectable mouth curved into a smile that encompassed both her mother and her. *I'm losing my mind.*

"Hello, Mrs. Kubek. Your relatives really know how to throw a wedding. I can't remember when I've had a better time." His fingers brushed Annie's, deliberately she thought, as he handed her a drink. "Or more beautiful company."

Wishing she liked the taste of alcohol more than she did, she tossed back a great quantity of ginger ale and choked when the mega-gulp caught in her throat.

"Easy, darlin'," Michael said, patting her on the back. Her eyes teared, but she wasn't sure whether it was from the ginger ale or frustration.

"She does look good in The Dress, doesn't she?" her mother said before Annie had recovered enough of her breath to speak.

"She most certainly does." Michael nodded while the polka band broke into another uproarious tune, and Annie gave her hemline another useless tug. "But why does everybody keep calling it *The Dress?*"

"Because it's the only one she has." Her mother

shook her head sadly. "Maybe you can take her shopping and get her to buy another one, Michael."

"I am not going shopping with—" Annie began.

"The two of you, you make the loveliest couple," her mother continued as though Annie hadn't spoken. "I can't wait to see you take a whirl around the dance floor."

"You're going to wait a long time if the band doesn't play something besides polkas," Michael said, smiling easily. "I don't know how to polka."

"Then Annie will teach you." Before Annie could say she wouldn't do any such thing, her mother's eyes widened in pleasure. "Oh, there's your mother, Michael. I need to speak to her. You two don't want an old woman in the way anyhow. Annie, teach Michael to polka."

Just then, on the dance floor, Uncle Janos gave Aunt Eugenia such a vigorous turn that she nearly plowed into them. Michael's arm came instantly around Annie, yanking her away from the pivoting couple so that her back came flat against his chest. It felt solid and warm, but Annie was sure she could find something wrong with it if she had enough time.

"Sorry, Annie," Aunt Eugenia yelled as she whirled past. "Good thing you have a *kochanie* to save you."

"What's a *kochanie?*" Michael asked. Annie scowled, unwilling to provide the answer. Michael didn't know a whit of Polish, so she didn't have to. Any answer she gave would satisfy him.

"I'll tell you if you get your arm off me," she said, trying to sound cross. Instead, she sounded breathless. Across the dance floor, her mother had Christine

Reeves by the hand and was pointing in their direction. Their smiles looked smug. "Honestly, Michael, if you don't stop touching me our mothers are going to think their plan is working."

"Is that why you kept inching away from me during the church ceremony?" he asked, his arm still in place. His breath rustled her hair. "When the bride and groom walked down the aisle after it was all over, you were sitting so close to the end of the pew I thought her skirt was going to knock you over."

"Smart aleck," she said under her breath and spun out of his grasp as easily as the dancers on the floor maneuvered their turns. For the life of her, she couldn't understand why he was teasing her this way. It was almost as though his mother had enlisted him as a party of the pact. "We have to be united on this, Michael. Which means we can't give our mothers any encouragement. So you can't touch me."

"How are we going to dance if I can't touch you?" he asked with annoying logic, capturing her hand and drawing her out on the dance floor. "Now tell me what to do."

Click your heels together three times and say you want to go back to Los Angeles, Annie thought, but didn't say it. Technically, it wasn't his fault that he couldn't polka. She just didn't understand why she had to be the one to teach him. She sighed. She didn't understand why she'd gotten Rose Kubek as a mother, either.

"Hold my left hand with your right hand, and put your left hand on my waist," Annie said. He was already holding her hand, so he pulled her to him and encircled her waist so her body was flush against his.

"Like this?" he whispered as his breath rustled her hair and his lips grazed her temple.

"No. Not like that." She narrowed her eyes as she gazed up at him. She expected his eyes to be laughing, but instead they'd darkened to an even more ridiculous shade of green. "You're supposed to hold me *loosely* around the waist."

"Oh," he said, sounding as disappointed as she assured herself she wasn't. His grip loosened, and she concentrated on the burgundy and gray swirls in his tie.

"Now you take one big step and then two smaller ones, and you do it with alternating feet. Like this. *Right* two three. *Left* two three."

"I think I've got it," Michael said after a moment, grinning as he executed the step with such perfect precision they were gliding across the floor with the rest of the dancing couples.

"Then, you—"

Before Annie could tell him how to turn, he swung her in an arc worthy of a dancer from the old country. He picked up the lively rhythm as though he'd been born with the tune in his blood, whirling and twirling until she was breathless.

"Annie," a voice shouted above the music. Mary Moronsk, her third cousin twice removed by marriage, whizzed by. Her face was flushed red from exertion and her salt-and-pepper hair was nearly standing on end. "It's about time you got yourself a *kochanie*."

"You still haven't told me what that means," Michael

pointed out as he swung her in another graceful arc.

"It's Polish for somebody who doesn't step on your toes when you're dancing." Annie said the first thing that came to mind.

He tilted his blond head and looked at her skeptically.

"The polka's not an easy dance," she continued, embellishing her story. "I danced with so many men who weren't *kochanies* at the last wedding that my toes were black-and-blue for days."

She ignored the guilt that always stabbed at her when she lied, rationalizing that this lie was justified.

After everything else that had happened at this wedding, she was simply not going to tell him that *kochanie* was Polish for sweetheart.

Annie crossed her arms over her chest as she watched Michael polka with the latest in a long line of her female relatives. They thought nothing of tapping each other on the shoulder so they could cut in on a man who was, after all, her date.

Not that dance-happy Michael seemed to mind. He was acting, Annie thought crossly, exactly like a Polish Fred Astaire.

"Why the long face, sis? Don't tell me you're jealous because your future husband is dancing with Grandma Kubek?"

As Joe sat down next to her at the otherwise-deserted table, Annie glanced at him long enough to pick up the teasing glint in his dark eyes. She looked back at the dance floor, immediately focusing on Michael and their tiny, white-haired grandmother. Grandma Kubek was laughing so uproariously it looked as though Michael was having trouble holding her upright.

"Don't you dare try to get a rise out of me, Joe. You know the only place Michael is my future husband is in Mom's deluded mind. I'm not sure I even like the man."

"Then why were you kissing him?"

"Oh, no." Annie rolled her eyes and groaned. "Did Aunt Marta tell you, too?"

"Aunt Marta?" Joe shook his head, smiling so boyishly Annie was reminded of the little brother who used to sneak into her room to read her diary. "No, she didn't tell me. Uncle Andrew did."

"Uncle Andrew? But he wasn't anywhere near . . ." Annie began, then shook her head. "Oh, never mind. The Three Musketeers would love this family."

"I don't get your drift."

"You know: All for one, one for all. In this family, the eyes and ears of one are the eyes and ears of all."

On the dance floor, Grandma Kubek's mouth was open so wide in laughter that the gap where her teeth should have been was plainly visible. Joe nodded to the glass on the table between them. It contained a plate of white dentures floating in water.

"I can live with the eye and ear thing, but I don't want to have to start sharing teeth. I know Grandma says the false ones get uncomfortable, but she shouldn't take her teeth out if she plans on laughing like that."

"Why is she laughing like that?" Annie noticed that

Michael didn't seem to understand the joke either. He was gazing at the old woman with a worried look, as though wondering whether her aged heart could take so much jocularity. "What could possibly be so funny?"

"I don't know," Joe said, "but I heard Michael say something really odd to her before they started dancing. He said that Grandma shouldn't worry about wearing sandals. Then he used some word that sounded Polish, but I wasn't sure of the meaning."

The table where Annie and Joe were sitting was on the edge of the dance floor, and Michael swirled Grandma around and around until she was within a few feet of them. She caught her grandchildren's eyes as she passed by.

"My *kochanie,*" she shouted gaily as she flapped her toothless gums. "He said he'd be my *kochanie.*"

Laughter erupted from Annie, and she covered her mouth with her hand as she thought of the unwitting pass Michael had made at her eighty-year-old grandmother. Joe gazed at her with incomprehension, which Annie thought served him right for not bothering to learn any of the Polish words her parents bandied about.

Through tears of laughter, Annie watched Michael leave her still-hysterical grandmother when the song ended and walk purposefully to where she and Joe sat.

"Why do I get the feeling," he asked levelly, "that *kochanie* does not mean one who dances without stepping on his partner's toes?"

Annie laughed harder, enjoying herself more than she had since they entered the reception hall. She thought she saw a corner of Michael's mouth lift but didn't have time to give him credit for having a sense of humor, because her mother appeared in front of her like a specter of bad tidings. She grabbed Annie's hand and pulled her out of her chair.

"Let's go," she said, dragging her away from the two men. Annie had to fight to keep her balance as they walked. "It's time for Walter's bride to throw the bouquet. You're destined to catch it, so you need to get there early to get a good spot."

"Oh, Mom," Annie wailed, "I am not going to catch the bouquet. I don't want to be the next one to get married."

Her mother ignored her, keeping a death grip on her hand. She pulled her across the dance floor to the area where the single women were gathering for what Annie thought was the most ridiculous custom imaginable. As though catching a bunch of flowers portended marriage.

She blew out a breath, debated whether to make a dash for the exit, and decided against it. Just because she was lining up in the group of women vying for the bouquet didn't mean she had to catch it. She had free will. Instead of throwing her mother into hysterics by refusing to take part in the silly ceremony, she'd simply make sure she came away bouquet-less.

Annie knew from observation that most brides made such poor tosses the bouquet ended up on the floor directly behind them. Traditionally, the women in the first row then made a mad scramble to recover it.

She took a good look at the woman whom cousin Walter had married and concluded that not catching the bouquet would be a cinch. The bride wasn't much more than five feet tall, and she probably didn't weigh one hundred pounds.

Annie backed up a good ten feet behind the rest of the crowd as the drum roll that signaled the start of the ritual began. She could pick out her second-cousin Ursula's frizzy blond hair through the crowd of women. Ursula, in prime position directly behind the bride, was bouncing up and down.

"Throw it to me," Ursula shouted, thrusting her elbows out so nobody could get close to her. "Throw it to me!"

Annie giggled, thinking Ursula was a lock to make the catch. She ignored her mother's frantic arm motions signaling her to move forward, noting happily that she was closer to the crowd that had gathered to watch the ridiculous display than she was to the bride. At her mother's side, Joe and Michael watched with similar amused expressions.

The bride turned her back to the group. "I'm going to throw on the count of three," she announced loudly. "One, two, three!"

She extended her thin arm in front of her, bent it over the back of her head, and gave a great heave. The bouquet sailed into the air at least six feet above the heads of the screaming women in front of Annie and began its descent.

She looked up, her gaze locking on a harrowing swirl of pink and purple flowers. Her mother's smiling face seemed to appear among the blossoms.

"No!" Annie yelled at the catapulting vision of dread. She swung her arm so viciously that it connected with the end of the bouquet and sent it hurtling into the crowd of spectators.

She turned and watched in horror as it spiraled, pink and purple, end over end, straight toward the only person in the hall who she wanted to catch the bouquet even less than she did herself.

Michael grabbed the bouquet out of the air with a deft, athletic move of which she hadn't thought him capable. Hoots and hollers filled the hall as his eyes locked on hers. She willed him to stay where he was, but he walked toward her with that loose-limbed purposeful gait she had actually been starting to find attractive.

Then he stopped, smiled into her eyes, and bowed.

"I think this belongs to you," he said as he twirled the bouquet with a flourish. When he handed it to her, she was so stunned that she took it.

"You can't fight destiny," she heard her mother yell as her heart sunk to her toes. Annie closed her eyes, but she couldn't shut out the cheering of the crowd.

Chapter Six

Michael whistled as he walked up the dirt path to the Green Forest Nature Center, relishing the role of white knight in which his mother and Mrs. Kubek had cast him.

He tossed the keys to the Lexus he'd rented in the air and caught them, thinking that he had the keys to Annie's forgiveness in his hand.

Funny how a couple of jars of homemade jam could help get him out of his own jam. He'd driven his mother to the Kubeks to deliver the jam, arriving at the precise moment Annie phoned to say her pickup wouldn't start.

Both Mrs. Kubek and his mother had practically pushed him out the door, lending credence to Annie's contention that they were matchmaking. Michael hadn't minded, though, because he was ready for Annie to stop being angry with him.

Three whole days had gone by since Walter's blast of a wedding. He'd spent the time working the kinks out of the software Joe was designing and giving Annie time to cool off.

The time, he figured, was up. He didn't think Annie had been warranted in refusing to speak to him during the ride home from the wedding. Nor had he deserved to have her front door slammed shut in his face. Or to have her hang up on him the last three times he'd phoned.

It wasn't as though he'd told her relatives he didn't like the pastries they'd set out on the dessert table. All he'd done was play the part of the attentive boyfriend, which wasn't nearly as serious an offense.

He was ready to be forgiven, which was a pretty good bet considering he was her transportation home. Maybe she'd even kiss him in gratitude.

He smiled when he thought of the way she kissed him, and his spirits lifted. This anger thing was just a minor setback. If she could kiss him like that, it couldn't be long before she'd eat every one of those insulting words she'd thrown at him about not being her type.

Dusk was settling on the park like a thick dark cloud. He figured most of the employees had knocked off for the day when he found the nature center building empty aside from a few aquariums full of snakes and the pelts of various wild animals. He walked through the building and back into the twilight, not stopping until he came to a group of Girl Scouts clustered around the cages that held the raptors.

Annie was at the center of them, once more dressed in standard-issue shirt and trousers. The sun had nearly disappeared beneath the horizon, but her eyes were shaded by a wide-brimmed hat that couldn't quite hide the spark of life in them as she related Mr. Hoots's history to the group. Her stance was confident, her voice animated.

Michael hung back and watched her. She'd looked so stunning at the wedding that he couldn't take his eyes off her. He still couldn't stop staring at her.

"Soon it'll be too dark to see, so I only have time for one more question," she said. She hadn't given any indication that she'd seen him, but Michael was certain by the slight tightening of her jaw that she was aware of his presence.

One of the girls immediately raised her hand. "What's the owl's name?" she asked, indicating Mr. Hoots.

"His name?" Annie shook her head gravely. "We don't name the wild things here. He's a great horned owl, not a pet."

"But he's so cute," the girl said in protest as Mr. Hoots hopped around the cage and hooted.

"That's the kind of thinking that can get you in trouble. If you come upon an injured raptor in the wild, it's very important to remember that. They may look harmless, but their beaks and talons are sharp. Don't make the mistake of naming them and taking them home to play with."

Michael's grin grew as he watched the group disperse while Annie hung back and answered a few more stray questions. He was positive she was aware of him now, because she studiously avoided looking in his direction. He waited until all the scouts had gone to make his approach.

"Don't you know what happens to women who tell lies to children?" He didn't wait for an answer. "Like Pinocchio's, their noses grow and grow and grow."

She touched the turned-up end of her nose, which was still as small and as cute as it had been a few minutes before. Then she scowled, her standard expression as far as he was concerned.

"That's rich coming from you," she all but hissed. "I don't know where you get the nerve to lecture me on honesty after you invited yourself to Walter's wedding and then tricked my relatives into thinking we're romantically involved."

"Wait just a minute." Michael had been ready to apologize for what wasn't his fault, but he wasn't prepared to be maligned. "Your mother invited me, and I didn't trick anybody into believing anything. All I did was act like an attentive escort."

"You kept putting your arm around me, you danced too close to me, you called me beautiful, and then you kissed me in front of a table full of my relatives!" she shouted.

"You kissed me back!"

"If I did, it was only because I drank too much."

"You were drinking ginger ale!"

"Then you actually had the nerve," she said, completely ignoring his disclaimer, "to catch the bouquet and present it to me."

"I wouldn't have caught it if you hadn't acted like Babe Ruth and taken such a vicious swipe at it!"

She ignored that, too. "Don't you dare confuse the issue. It's your fault everybody in this entire town thinks we're getting married!"

Michael was about to issue another thunderous retort when her meaning got through to him. The problem was that her logic was off. Statement B didn't logically follow statement A.

"That's ridiculous. Nobody thinks we're getting married."

Her jaw clenched before she threw up her hands and stalked off. Michael stood watching her, scratching his jaw, wondering how that could possibly have gone so wrong.

He'd come to apologize, and she was even angrier than she had been in the aftermath of the bouquet fiasco.

"Would it help if I said I was sorry?" he called after her, but she continued on as if she hadn't heard him. He was tempted to rush after her and make her listen, but then he reminded himself there was no need to rush. With a broken-down truck, Annie wasn't going anywhere without him.

"Would it help if I said I was sorry?" Annie bit out under her breath in an imitation of Michael's perfectly cultured voice as she stalked away. "Nothing's going to help until you get out of Dodge. There's not room in this town for the both of us."

As she muttered the answer, she kicked a rock with such gusto it boomeranged off a tree and struck her a smarting blow to the thigh. She yelped and rubbed the sore area as she walked.

"That's great," she said sarcastically as she burst through the doors of the nature center, her thigh still smarting. "Just great."

Not only had Michael Reeves so exasperated her that she was sending flying projectiles her own way, but he also had her talking to herself and providing the answers. If she didn't watch it, she'd resurrect her imaginary childhood playmate and ask if she'd help her pick out a new dress.

"What are you doin' here so late, Annie?"

The voice of Lou Spinelli, the park manager, was more annoying than startling. She wasn't in the mood to deal with his very real threats to recommend that the park system strip her of the funding she needed to keep the raptors.

"I told you this afternoon I'd be here late." Annie walked from the main part of the building to the reception area near the front door. Lou followed her, his arms crossed over his chest, gnawing on that infernal wintergreen gum. "Some Girl Scouts asked if they could come in after hours, so I stayed late to show them the raptors."

She put the receptionist's desk between them and turned to regard him. With his dimples, big brown eyes, and air of an All-American boy, Lou looked as though he'd be the perfect cast member for a television sitcom. He certainly didn't resemble the rat that he was.

"Forget about putting in for overtime. I'm not approving extra pay for something you could have scheduled during park hours. Anything you do after five o'clock, you do on your own time."

Annie bit back a sarcastic retort and made herself speak in a normal tone. "I didn't plan on putting in for overtime. But I also wasn't going to turn away a group of children interested in learning about raptors. That's why I'm here, Lou. To teach others about the birds so they can appreciate them as much as I do."

"You're still fighting for those birds then?"

"Till my dying day," she said levelly. "But then you already know that."

He brushed back the chestnut-colored bangs that fell artfully across his forehead, and his brown eyes gleamed. "You've made some bad choices in your life, Annie, if you're spending the night with a bunch of birds."

It took everything in Annie's power not to roll her eyes in disgust. Lou Spinelli had the most severe case of arrested development she'd ever encountered. He seemed stuck back in high school, when he'd spread rumors about her because she refused to go out with him. She got ready to blast him when she remembered her predicament.

Until she figured out exactly how to save her birds, antagonizing him would be foolish. The county was so desperate to slash spending she had little doubt that a park manager's suggestion to do away with one of his own programs would be taken seriously.

"I'm not going to spend the night at the park, Lou. I'm only still here because the battery in my pickup's dead."

"How'd a self-sufficient feminist like you let that

happen, Annie?" He walked purposely around the desk to where Annie stood, which was more irritating than frightening. She'd been handling Lou Spinelli since he was a pimply-faced adolescent, and she had little doubt she could do so now. The difference was that now, as never before, she had to use tact. "Don't you know that a woman can't be too careful these days?"

"Neither can a man," came a steel-edged voice from behind Lou. "Because if you don't move away from her in the next second, you're going to be sorry you ever dared speak to her."

Michael! Annie's gaze swung from Lou to the stern-jawed, icy-eyed, uninformed fool introducing yet another unwanted complication into her life. After their confrontation by the raptor cages, she'd hoped he'd gotten into his pretentious car and driven away. Instead, darn it, he'd followed her.

"Are you threatening me?" Lou asked incredulously.

"That's exactly what I'm doing," Michael answered in a voice so unlike his cultivated own that Annie was struck momentarily speechless.

"Just who do you think you are?"

Michael smiled through his anger, which produced such a menacing picture that the shape of Annie's eyes reconformed into the O her mouth was making. "I'm the man who doesn't need much more of an excuse to realign your nose."

A mental image of her raptors being carted off in cages for parts unknown flashed before her widened eyes, and Annie blanched. If she didn't do something fast, her birds were as good as gone. The thought prompted her into action. She edged around Lou and hurried to Michael's side, placing a restraining hand on his arm. The muscles in it were coiled.

"Stop it, Michael." She desperately tried to signal with her eyes that she neither wanted nor needed him to come to her defense. "You've misread the situation here."

"I haven't misread anything," he said, his words clipped and his angry stare still directed at Lou. "I'm not going to stand around and listen to some imbecile threaten—"

"This imb . . . I mean man, is my boss," Annie interrupted.

"Your boss?"

"Yes, my boss," she repeated, capitalizing on the fact that some of Michael's anger seemed to have rechanneled into shock. "Michael, meet Lou Spinelli, the park manager. Lou, this is Michael Reeves, a friend of the family's."

Neither man offered to shake hands, causing Annie's stomach to plunge. Her only hope was to get Michael away from Lou before he could cause any more damage to the fate of her birds.

"Before we were so rudely interrupted," Lou began, causing Annie to think the damage might already have been done, "I was about to offer you a ride home, Annie."

"Forget it. *I'm* driving her home," Michael bit out, as though he were one of two dogs fighting over a bone. Unfortunately, that bone was her. Even more unfortunately, Annie couldn't argue. Michael was incredibly annoying, but he was still preferable to Lou.

"Thanks for the offer, but I wouldn't want to put you to any trouble." Annie's hand was still on Michael's arm, and she guided him firmly toward the door, aware that the tension inside of him hadn't dissipated. "We've got to be going, but I'll see you tomorrow, Lou. You'll lock up, won't you?"

Lou muttered something that sounded like agreement, and Annie pushed open the door, almost shoving Michael through it. Because she couldn't yet trust herself to speak in a voice lower than a yell, she moved swiftly down the path that led to the gravel parking lot, trying to get out of Lou's earshot.

"What was that all about?" Michael asked angrily.

Annie kept walking, not trusting herself to answer.

"That man acted like a first-rate jerk," he continued, "and when I tried to take him to task for it, you practically kissed his hand. It's like you didn't even notice he was way out of line."

Annie stopped so abruptly Michael would have careened into her if he hadn't danced off to the side of the path. Twigs and leaves crunched under his feet, and he just barely avoided hitting his forehead on a low-hanging tree branch.

"Of course I noticed," Annie hissed, "but that doesn't mean I needed you to perform a Tarzan-to-the-rescue act. Especially because we both know you wouldn't have hit him."

"You're not making sense."

"That's because you think nothing of coming into my life and turning everything completely upside down and inside out. Didn't it occur to you that I might have a reason for not wanting to antagonize my boss? Didn't you think before you issued your empty threats?"

"First of all, they weren't empty threats," Michael said as though he actually expected her to believe he would have cocked his cultured fist and punched Lou in the nose with it. "And secondly, you don't have to put up with talk like that just because he's your boss."

"I do if I don't want to lose my birds, and that's exactly what'll happen if he recommends to the county that our funding be cut."

"But why would he do that? From what I can see, you're providing the public with a valuable educational service."

"Do you think that matters to somebody like Lou?" Annie tried to contain her anger. It didn't work. Self-restraint, after all, had never been one of her strengths.

"What does matter to him?"

"Revenge!"

"Revenge?"

"Yes, revenge. He wants to make me pay for refusing to go out with him the last twenty times he asked."

"Then file a sexual-harassment suit."

Annie shook her head. "You don't understand anything."

"Then explain it to me."

"A sexual-harassment suit wouldn't stick."

"Why not?"

"Because the first time Lou asked me out, I was fifteen. The last time, I was a senior in high school. He doesn't want to go out with me anymore. He wants me to pay for not wanting to go out with him.

"Which is why," she narrowed her eyes at him, "I can't afford to antagonize him."

"I wasn't antagonizing him," Michael said. "I was threatening him."

Annie looked as though she were about to say something else. But then, for the second time that day, she pivoted on her heels and stamped away from him. Michael put his hands on his hips. He couldn't win with Annie no matter what he did.

He'd reacted instead of thought when he came across that scene in the nature center, but he wouldn't have acted any differently had he known the circumstances. He couldn't have stood idly by while Lou Spinelli threatened her, even if the man were her boss. There had to be another way Annie could keep her raptors without having to kowtow to him. Michael felt sure he could come up with it once he had time to think the situation through.

In the meantime, darn it, he would too have punched the other man in his supercilious little nose. No matter what Annie thought.

He followed Annie to the parking lot, concentrating on how he was going to get her home in relative peace. When he got there, he saw that wasn't going to happen. Annie, anger radiating from every pore, was trying to yank open the passenger door.

"This isn't California," she bit out. "Why did you lock the door? Did you think Yogi Bear was going to come to life and try to steal your precious Lexus? I'll tell you something. This car is so pretentious that Yogi wouldn't even want it."

Michael's temper flared at the unfairness of her latest attack. "Oh, yeah. Well, even Boo-Boo wouldn't want your broken-down, rusted-out pickup truck."

Michael indicated the ancient vehicle next to his with the sweep of his hand. He fished his remote out of his pocket and pressed the button that unlocked the car doors. She got in without another word, leaving Michael standing in front of the Lexus, feeling ashamed.

Why had he let himself be baited into arguing with her? He'd come to the park a short time ago hopeful that she was ready to be friends—well, okay, *more* than friends—and here he was shouting at her in a parking lot.

Worse, he'd been shouting at her that Yogi Bear's sidekick Boo-Boo would rather drive a Lexus than an old pickup.

The thought was almost as ludicrous as Annie's declaration that everyone in Elmwood thought they were getting married because he'd caught the bridal bouquet. He let out a long breath until his temper receded back to its normal state. Then he got into the car.

Annie was still so angry he wouldn't have been surprised had the windows steamed, but she seemed resigned to riding the ten miles back to town with him. That, more than anything, told him how she felt about Lou Spinelli.

He turned the key in the ignition, resolving not to be drawn into another argument. He'd concentrate on negotiating the winding country road while she regained enough composure to discuss their differences in a rational manner.

Five miles into the trip, he drummed his fingers on the steering wheel while the silence screamed in his ears. He couldn't take another second of it.

"You know, of course," she muttered an instant before he would have spoken, "that our situation is only going to get worse if Lou tells anybody about the Tarzan act you pulled back at the park."

"What situation?"

"What situation?" she repeated with asperity. "The everybody-in-Elmwood-thinks-we're-getting-married situation, that's what situation."

"You're overreacting. Nobody thinks we're getting married," Michael said as calmly and as logically as he knew how. "Nobody actually believes the person who catches the bouquet at a wedding will be the next one married."

"Our mothers believe it!" Annie said. "They thought we were destined for each other before either one of us even touched the bouquet! Now that we both did, they probably believe in the pact even more fervently."

"Would you cut it out with that pact stuff," Michael said irritably, unwilling to listen to another ridiculous rendition of her baby-betrothal story, especially since it concerned his mother. "Besides, even if your mother does believe it, nobody else does."

"Are you kidding? Everybody else believes it. Even before you caught the bouquet, my mother was telling everybody you were my fiancé. Are you so super-cosmopolitan that you have no idea how a small town works? I haven't been able to go anywhere in the past three days without somebody asking me when the wedding is."

"You're exaggerating."

"Oh, yeah? Then why did the bridal shop call yesterday to ask me to come in for a fitting? And why does the bakery want to know whether I want to order chocolate filling for a white cake or vanilla filling for a chocolate cake? And why does the florist want me to choose between carnations and mums?"

They were nearing the top of a mountain. To the side of the road was a dirt-and-gravel clearing that afforded a magnificent view of the valley below. Michael swung the car off the road, his tires spitting gravel as he veered. He shut off the engine, ignored the view, and looked at Annie.

"I must have missed something. Are you actually saying that the bridal shop, the florist, and the bakery have been phoning you?"

Her brown eyes narrowed. She took off her hat, ruffling her short, dark hair as she did so. It fell in disheveled curls around her flushed face.

"Yes." She shook her head as though he mystified her. "What do you think I've been trying to tell you for the past half hour? The whole town thinks we're engaged."

Michael rubbed his chin and shook his head as he tried to take in enough air, but even colossal gulps of oxygen couldn't erase the horror of the word "engaged."

He did not, under any circumstance, want that word associated with him. Even if marriage had been one of his goals, which it most definitely was not, he didn't want a serious relationship.

He spent the great bulk of his time either on the

phone or chained to his computer. At the end of the year, he fully expected to become a CompTech vice president. After that, he could pick whichever path he wanted to take. It certainly wouldn't be down the altar.

"I am not getting married," he stated, feeling better now that he'd said the words aloud. Annie was making too much of what had happened at the wedding. Still, the statement bore repeating. "I am *not* getting married."

Chapter Seven

"**I** heard you say you weren't getting married the first time." Annie frowned at him. He was shaking his head, as though the very idea of marriage was terrifying. "Since I have no intention of getting married either, what are we going to do about this mess we're in?"

"What mess?"

"Honestly, Michael. Haven't you been listening to me at all? Everybody in Elmwood, my mother foremost among them, thinks we're getting married. We have to come up with a way to change their way of thinking."

Michael scratched his head. "Why don't we just tell them we're not getting married?"

Annie harrumphed. "As though that would work.

100

I've been telling my mother I'm not going to marry you since I've been about five years old, and it's never dissuaded her before. Did you know she's even picked out a wedding date?"

"She what?"

"She thinks we should get married the first weekend in August."

"Since we don't think so, I don't understand why that's a problem."

"Are you kidding? You've met my mother. When she gets hold of an idea, she's like a dog with a bone. Think of this wedding thing as the bone. She won't let go unless we yank it out of her mouth. We have to think up something to get that bone away from her. Something drastic."

His green eyes twinkled, which Annie didn't understand considering the gravity of the subject. "I hope," he said, as his beautiful mouth curved into a smile, "that you're not proposing a visit to the dog pound."

"Stop joking, Michael. This is serious."

"So what do you propose then?"

"I don't suppose you could cut your trip short." He gave her a wry look. "No? In that case, our best bet is for you to date somebody else while you're here. Let me think for a minute who I could set you up with. I know. How about my cousin Ursula?" Annie ignored the way her stomach clenched at the thought of Michael and her cousin and plunged ahead. "You probably remember her from the wedding. She's about my height and she has miles of frizzy blond hair."

"Oh, no, you don't." Michael shook his head vigorously. The laughter in his too-green eyes was gone, replaced, she thought, by panic. "She's the one who was yelling for the bride to throw her the bouquet. I'm not getting near anybody who's that desperate to get married."

Annie thought of the white wedding dress already hanging in Ursula's closet and briefly wondered at the crap shoot that was life. Marriage-minded Ursula would have been perfectly happy with Rose Kubek as a mother. But, no. Annie had to get Rose instead. "I suppose you have a point. Just give me a couple of minutes, and I'll come up with somebody else."

"No," Michael said forcefully. "I don't have the time to date anybody. If I did, I want to do the choosing. Besides, you're being ridiculous. So what if the people around here think we're getting married? We know we're not."

"That's not good enough." Annie shook her head.

"Why not? Nobody can make us get married."

"I guess that's true," Annie said slowly and looked at him. That was a mistake. She couldn't deny the appeal of the well-groomed, Armani-wearing version of Michael that had charmed everybody at Walter's wedding, but she much preferred this rendition. Everything about him was a little rumpled, from his hair to the khakis and sports shirt that stretched across his surprisingly broad chest. She even thought she saw the beginning of some blond stubble on his chin, which made his too-straight nose and too-high cheekbones more acceptable.

"Especially when you're about the last woman in the world I'd marry," he said and then added hastily.

"That is, of course, if I were getting married in the first place."

Annie was uncomfortably aware that she'd said something similar to him barely a week before. She'd even been giggling as she said it, although he hadn't seemed to find the situation nearly as humorous as she had. She wasn't laughing now.

She clenched her teeth, telling herself his opinion didn't matter in the slightest, telling herself she was not, under any circumstances, going to ask what he meant. She didn't want to marry him. He lived in Los Angeles, for goodness sake. He wore designer clothes.

"Why wouldn't you want to marry me?" she heard herself ask. To her horror, he laughed. It wasn't long and it wasn't loud, but it was definitely a laugh.

"You're kidding, right?" He looked at her with raised eyebrows a few shades darker than his hair. They were nice eyebrows, she thought idly, forgetting that she didn't like anything about him. Thankfully, he reminded her. "You can come up with an entire list of reasons you don't want to marry me. What makes you think I can't do the same for you?"

Annie frowned. The words "poetic justice" came to mind, but she quickly banished them. He was bluffing. He had to be. Just because she could come up with an abundance of reasons he was unsuitable didn't mean he could do the same thing. He'd already told her she impressed him as a no-frills woman who didn't care what anybody thought of her, but those weren't reasons not to marry somebody.

"What are they?" she asked, a challenge in her voice.

"I don't think I should tell you." He shook his head, and for some reason her eyes dipped to his mouth. Full lips shouldn't look good on á man, but his did. She jerked her eyes up. "Who knows what you'd do if I told you. You're way too temperamental."

Annie gritted her teeth, annoyed at him for baiting her and at herself for staring at his mouth. "Tell me," she ordered.

"Well, for starters," he said and grinned. "You're way too temperamental. I like my women with sweeter dispositions."

"You mean you like women who wouldn't dream of disagreeing with anything that comes out of your luscious mouth," Annie shot back.

"You think my mouth is luscious?" Too late, Annie realized what she'd said and covered her own mouth. Darn it all. She should have known that the bewildering fixation she had on his mouth would get her into this kind of trouble.

"I didn't mean luscious in a good way," she said, and he looked at her uncomprehendingly. She couldn't explain what she meant, even to herself, so she decided to sidetrack him.

"Don't stop now," she ordered. "I want to hear the other reasons you don't want to marry me."

"No, you don't."

"I most certainly do want to hear your other reasons. You started this conversation. The least you could do is have the decency to finish it."

"Okay, then. You're much too argumentative."

"How can you say I'm argumentative? I'm nothing of the kind," Annie retorted, and he threw his head back and laughed. She bit her lip, realizing she had walked right into his trap.

"You're also prejudiced—"

"I am not prejudiced," she denied hotly.

"—against cosmopolitan men who grew up in Europe and have blond hair and green eyes."

"I guess I can't argue too much with that one," she conceded, feeling a grin sneaking across her lips. She could live with the fact that he thought her temperamental, argumentative, and prejudiced against blond men. She didn't think any of those qualities were particularly negative. "If that's all you can find wrong with me, I guess I should be flattered."

"I didn't say that's all I can find wrong with you."

"You mean there's more?" She bit her lip, hurt. "How could there be more?"

"We haven't discussed your clothes yet." He wiggled his perfect eyebrows. "Aside from that dress you wore to the wedding, they are sorely lacking in brevity."

Her face reddened until she saw that his lips were quivering with barely controlled laughter.

"Now you're teasing me," she accused, and he let out a guffaw.

"That's only because you look cute when you blush. I would have used the word beautiful, by the way, if I didn't already know how angry it makes you when I say it."

"It makes me angry when you say it around other people," she corrected with a burst of honesty. "It wouldn't make me angry if you said it now."

"It wouldn't?"

The laughter died on her lips, and she thought she had very possibly said the wrong thing. "Every woman likes to hear she's beautiful," Annie said, because she couldn't very well deny something that was true. "Even if the man doesn't mean it."

"What makes you think I don't mean it?" He shifted in his leather seat and brushed her disheveled hair back from her face. She might have mustered the will to bat his hands away if her eyes hadn't focused on his mouth again. She'd really developed a thing for his mouth.

She cleared her suddenly clogged throat. "How could you mean it when you just spent fifteen minutes telling me why I didn't attract you?"

"No." He shook his head while he played with the ends of her hair. "I just spent fifteen minutes telling you why I didn't want to *marry* you. Believe me, I'm plenty attracted to you."

Her voice cracked. "You are?"

"Oh, yes. Very attracted."

Annie nervously licked her lips and then realized she'd made a mistake when his gaze centered on them. She closed her eyes. This was worse than ridiculous. This man had been making her life unbearable, albeit unwittingly, for the past twenty-some years, and she wanted nothing more than to kiss him.

"Do you know where we are?" she asked shakily.

His hand moved from her hair to her cheek, and his smile touched his eyes. "On a mountaintop just outside of Elmwood?"

"All the teenagers call it Makeout Pass, because this is their favorite spot to, well, make out."

The darkness rose out of the valley to shadow Michael's too-pretentious rental car, but she could still see his eyes. In them was something gentle and tender and somehow real.

His other hand lifted so he was cupping both of her cheeks, and his eyes looked beautiful in the twilight. Like the grass on a velvety night. "Did you come here to make out when you were a teenager?"

"Only once." Annie smiled at the memory. "But Danny Morelli was so nervous he bit my lip, and it bled. That ruined the mood."

He laughed, a low sound that vibrated through her. "If I kiss you now, is Danny Morelli going to hunt me down later?"

"Unh-unh. Danny got married to Angie Novak right out of high school and has four kids." She lifted her eyes to his and swallowed. "But if you don't kiss me now, I might hunt you down later."

This time, Michael's smile reached all the way to his beautiful green eyes. Annie smiled back as her heart filled with something that felt suspiciously close to tenderness. She went willingly when he drew her face to his and kissed her.

The instant their mouths came together, Annie's entire body softened so that it felt like she was melting. She clutched at his shoulders, certain she wouldn't be able to hold herself up if she didn't have something to anchor her. His lips moved on hers in an unhurried exploration, kissing and tasting and teasing until she wound her hands around his neck.

His eyes were open, watching her. "I love the way

you kiss me," he murmured against her lips. "As though you never want me to stop."

"I don't," Annie confessed, beyond caring what she was admitting. For three days, she'd been so angry at him that she hadn't stopped to think about the meaning of the response he could so easily elicit. She hadn't let herself think about the way she'd kissed him at the wedding or, earlier, on the walking path the first night they'd met. She hadn't thought about anything but her anger, but now he was extinguishing that with his kiss.

A series of sharp noises, almost like the tapping of a woodpecker, invaded her brain. She dismissed the thought immediately, because a woodpecker wouldn't be tapping on Michael's Lexus. The sounds came again, more insistent this time, and she couldn't ignore them any longer.

Michael must have heard the raps, too, because he slowly broke off the kiss, affording her a clear view of the passenger-side window and the face of her seventeen-year-old cousin Jimmy.

He was waving and wearing an imagine-finding-you-here expression. Michael drew away from her and turned toward the window. The boy, who'd been at Walter's wedding, smashed his nose against the window so that it resembled a pig's snout and waved at him, too.

"Did you know that my cousin Jimmy is so stubborn he won't go away unless we wave back at him?" Annie asked, trying to pretend she wasn't embarrassed.

They both struggled to a sitting position and gave him weak waves. Jimmy grinned.

"Hey, Annie. Hey, Mr. Reeves. Nice running into you," he called through the closed window. He gave them a thumbs-up sign before retreating to the car neither of them had heard pull up. A teenage girl, one of the few people in town not related to Annie, sat in the front seat, craning her neck to get a better view of them.

Neither Annie nor Michael said anything until they had made their getaway and were heading back down the mountain toward Elmwood. Then they looked at each other and burst out laughing.

"We've really gone and done it this time," Annie said, laughing so hard that tears streamed down her face. "Jimmy's going to tell everyone he knows he saw us there together."

"Look on the bright side," Michael said, laughing so hard he could barely form words. "Maybe he won't want anyone to know he was at Makeout Pass."

"Are you kidding me? My family is as chauvinistic as the next family. It's the girls who don't want anyone to know they were at Makeout Pass. The boys shout it from the rooftops.

"Mark my words. By tomorrow, my mother will have heard about this. She'll be so concerned about my reputation that she'll want to move up the wedding date."

"We need to move up the wedding date."

Annie finished drying one of the dozens of dinner dishes her mother insisted wouldn't get clean in the dishwasher and looked toward the ceiling, not caring if her mother got a view of the whites of her eyes.

She'd been waiting through dinner, dessert, and cleanup for her mother to bring up the never-going-to-happen wedding. The fact that the older woman had waited until now to broach the subject churning Annie's insides heightened her annoyance level.

Annie blew out a breath that ruffled her bangs as she returned a frying pan to its place under the stove, banging so many other pots and pans in the process that she sounded like a drummer in a percussion band.

"If there were going to be a wedding, which there isn't, we wouldn't need to move up the date just because Jimmy caught Michael and me up at Makeout Pass."

Annie straightened just in time to see her mother let out a gasp worthy of a cartoon character and slap her hands to her cheeks. "Jimmy caught you and Michael at Makeout Pass?"

"Yes," Annie snapped, annoyed that her mother was pretending she didn't already know. "And no matter what you think, that is not further proof that we're getting married."

"Jimmy caught you and Michael at Makeout Pass," her mother repeated, but this time her voice was considering instead of theatrical. She removed her hands from her cheeks, which were reddened from the slap, and tapped a finger against her chin. "Exactly when was this?"

"After he picked me up yesterday. As if you didn't know," Annie answered, then studied her mother. Her expression was thoughtful, and she seemed to be digesting the information. A black wave of horror rolled over Annie. "Wait a minute. Don't tell me you didn't know I'd been up at Makeout Pass with Michael?"

"I know now," her mother answered as it struck Annie that she'd opened her mouth and stuck her boot-clad foot into it. "But now I'm even more worried than before. If you were with Michael last night, why did he go out to dinner with that woman?"

Her mother paused and wagged her finger, the way she used to when Annie wouldn't eat her vegetables. "You must not have let him kiss you."

"Of course I let him kiss me," Annie retorted. She didn't have time to become too horrified at herself for confirming that she'd kissed Michael, because part of what her mother had said belatedly sank into her befuddled brain.

"Woman? Did I just hear you say that Michael went out to dinner last night with another woman?"

"Yes," her mother confirmed. "Why did you think I told you we needed to move up the wedding date? I asked him last night if he wanted to stay for dinner, but he went out with this woman instead."

Annie's heart hurt, as though somebody had gotten a hammer and taken a mighty whack at it. "What woman?" she asked, and her voice sounded pitifully small.

"That new woman. What's the name of that place where she works? You know. The bird place." She flapped her arms as though ready to take flight. "With the veterinarians."

"You mean the raptor rehabilitation center?" Annie dropped her dish towel and walked to the kitchen table, where she sank into one of the upholstered chairs.

She was only aware of one woman who worked at the rehabilitation center. "Are you saying Michael went out to dinner last night with Felicity Pomposity?"

"I think her first name is Felicity, but that last name doesn't sound right." Her mother bit her lip. "Aunt Ida called me as soon as the mother of that little Spinelli girl who works at the Dew Drop Inn told her that they were there together. Aunt Ida said that Gladys Spinelli said that her daughter Doris said this Felicity was smiling at Michael like a piranha waiting to sink her teeth into him."

"That snake," Annie said under her breath, not even bothering to refute her mother's contention that killer fish could smile. How dare Michael insist he didn't have time to date anybody. Only he hadn't gone out with just anybody. He'd gone out with the woman who had been keeping her from her precious peregrine falcon. "How could he have gone out with Felicity Pomposity after what I told him? I've a mind to punch him in that perfect nose of his."

"This isn't good," her mother said, shaking her head. "I was going to move the wedding up to July when I heard about this Felicity, but now I'm thinking June. It won't be good for your reputation if you're seen kissing Michael while he's going out with other women."

Instead of denying there was anything in her future that would be old, new, borrowed, or blue or explaining that a woman of the new millennium had a perfect right to kiss anybody she chose, Annie fumed.

"Do you know what he whispered to me last night before he left?" Annie bristled as she thought of the way Michael's eyes had filled with pretend regret. "That the only thing that was going to get him through the *business* he had to take care of was thinking of me."

"Well, that's a good sign, but—"

"To think he was lying through those perfectly aligned teeth of his! Then he smiled his perfect smile at me! I don't think he's going to be smiling after I knock out a few of his ultra-white teeth!"

"Now, Annie." Her mother laid a hand on her shoulder. "If you break Michael's nose and knock out his teeth, he's not going to look too good on your wedding day. You don't look so good yourself right now. Your face is turning green. That's why jealousy is such an unattractive trait."

"I'm not jealous," Annie denied hotly. "I'm angry." She placed her hands on the kitchen table and shoved, getting to her feet.

"Where are you going?" her mother asked in alarm.

"Where do you think I'm going? I want to find out for myself just what Michael thinks he's doing."

"Don't do it, Annie," her mother warned. "You know how men are when you confront them."

Annie didn't reply. Her boots made heavy, thudding sounds as she traipsed to the front door and flung it open. Joe and Michael were playing basketball in the driveway. Darkness had already fallen, and the floodlight that Joe had set up over the detached garage illuminated the scene.

A basketball backboard was suspended over the garage, and four players were vying for a rebound. Michael and Joe were two of them. The others were

Andy and Jeff Pachowski, the two tallest and best players on Elmwood High's excellent basketball team.

With a jolt of astonishment, Annie watched Michael, who she felt sure was the weakest player of the four, come away with the rebound. He dribbled away from the other three, and she couldn't take her eyes off him.

It was an uncommonly warm night, and he wasn't wearing anything but a pair of gym shorts, athletic socks, and court shoes. His chest was amazingly developed, and his legs were sculpted with long, ropy muscles and dusted with fine golden hair.

He left the ground and let loose a perfectly arched jump shot that swished through the hoop without touching the rim. Then he raised his gorgeously developed arms to signal that his shot had been far enough away from the basket to be worth three points instead of two.

Joe was also shirtless, so she figured that he and Michael were teaming against the Pachowski brothers. The more talented Pachowski, the one Annie remembered as having scored thirty points in the last game she'd seen, drove to the basket and put up a shot. Michael not only rejected it, but managed to grab the ball in the ensuing scramble. Within seconds, he had scored again, this time on a turnaround one-handed sky hook.

"Lucky shot," one of the Pachowskis grumbled.

Joe laughed. "Then he's been lucky all night. We're creaming you guys."

From behind her, her mother said, "Leave the boys alone, Annie."

"Fat chance," Annie answered, but her mind was on Michael instead of her mother's order. Why had she thought he was too tall? The spindly Pachowski brothers, each of whom topped Michael by three or four inches, were too tall. Michael was the ideal height, with sculpted limbs in perfect proportion to the rest of him.

"He's such a handsome man that it would be a shame if you spoiled the wedding pictures," her mother said with a sense of urgency. "Keep that in mind if you hit him, Annie. Avoid his face or one day you'll have to explain to your grandchildren why your groom had a broken nose and missing teeth on your wedding day."

Her mother's chatter broke Annie out of her trance at the same time that Michael looked up to where they were standing on the porch. The fierce competitor's mask he'd been wearing a moment before disappeared, replaced by a smile as bright as the flood lights under which they played. He waved.

That did it for Annie. The snake was actually acting as though he were glad to see her not even twenty-four hours after he'd been spotted cavorting with her falcon-withholding enemy. She wasn't having any of it. She ran down the porch steps, her adrenaline pumping as fast as her feet as she prepared to do battle.

Michael, however, was still engaged in a contest of another sort. The basketball sailed toward him. He caught it easily, dribbling through his legs and behind his back before he drove to the basket, bumping bodies while he muscled his way to a lay-up.

Annie stopped in her pursuit—smack-dab in the

middle of their court—and her jaw dropped in awe. Cultured, sophisticated Michael Reeves actually seemed to have a touch of street smarts, at least when it came to basketball. She wouldn't have been more surprised if she'd found Michael Jordan playing in the shadow of her parents' house.

"Hey, sis," Joe yelled, annoyance edging his voice. His hands were on his hips, and he was breathing hard. "We're in the middle of a game here."

"Don't give her a hard time, Joe," Michael cut in before Annie could answer. He tossed the ball to Joe with the fluid confidence of an athlete. "I've had enough anyway. These kids are wearing me out."

Since he was barely sweating and wasn't even out of breath, that was obviously not true. The Pachowski teenagers protested, loudly demanding a chance to redeem themselves, and Michael promised them a rematch. Annie had come charging onto the court with a purpose, but she forgot what it was when Michael walked toward her.

"Where'd you learn to play like that?" She asked the first question that popped into her head. His chest hair was slightly darker than the hair on his head, reminding her of burnished wheat, and she wondered why she'd ever considered his blondness to be a negative trait.

"Believe it or not," he said easily as he came closer, "there are basketball courts in Europe where people like me can go when our too-cosmopolitan lifestyles get old."

Annie put her hands on her hips and glared at him. There was something about his flippant answer that

she didn't like, but she couldn't figure out what it was.
So she took the offensive. "If you don't watch out, I'll
tell you where you can go."

His easy demeanor disappeared into the night, and
he lowered his voice. He wasn't perspiring, but there
was something elemental and earthy about the way he
smelled. She drew in a deeper breath. "If you're getting ready to argue with me, Annie, I suggest you do
it in private. We have an audience."

For a moment, Annie was tempted not to argue with
him to prove that she wasn't argumentative, but then
thoughts of falcon-withholding Felicity Pomposity
flew back into her head. She whipped her head around
to see four pairs of interested eyes on them. He was
right. They couldn't have this argument in the glow
of the basketball court.

"Come on," she said, grabbing his hand.

Chapter Eight

Michael sent his three playing partners and a visibly distressed Mrs. Kubek an apologetic shrug and followed Annie. Her hair was a mass of hat-flattened curls, and she was wearing that awful park ranger's uniform, but darned if he didn't think she looked beautiful.

She was angry about something again. Her color was high, reddening her cheeks and giving the rest of her skin a luminous glow. The brown eyes that had glared at him a moment ago looked as bright as Independence Day sparklers.

The part of her that he was most interested in right now, however, was her brain. It was more fascinating than a complicated computer loaded with advanced software. He never knew what she was going to do or say next. From the look on her face, he was pretty sure she was angry at him for something. But, for the life of him, he couldn't figure out what.

"Are you going to tell me where we're going?" he asked when they were about thirty feet from her parents' front door. She neither let go of his hand nor broke stride.

"Privacy you wanted, privacy you're going to get," she said in clipped tones. "We're going to my place."

He was tempted to stop walking to force her to explain her inexplicable behavior, but he'd seen Annie's temper in action. If he refused to go along, chances were she'd yell at him in the middle of the street, where anybody could hear. Somehow, the fact that they were overheard would turn out to be his fault, too. So he let her lead the way, figuring it would be better if she vented in private.

A car door opened in a darkened driveway off to their left, and the glow of the vehicle's interior light illuminated a woman he recognized from the wedding. He never recognized anyone in Los Angeles. Gosh, he loved this town. He smiled and waved, and the woman returned the greeting.

The night air felt cool against his slightly damp skin, reminding Michael that he wasn't wearing a shirt. He thought of the sight they must present. He was bare-chested, and Annie was dragging him by the hand through the streets of Elmwood. Everyone was so interested in Annie and him that he could imagine the kinds of tales that would be flowing through town tomorrow. Maybe there'd even be a newspaper story with the headline, *Local Girl Resorts to Ways of Caveman to Get Her Guy.*

In less than a minute, they reached the small ranch house where she lived. It bore a startling resemblance to his mother's, except for the doormat that depicted a cartoon bubble suspended over a fierce-eyed hawk saying WELCOME.

Annie yanked open the door, which she hadn't bothered to lock, and pulled him into the darkened interior.

"Now are you going to tell me what's wrong?" he asked as she flipped on the hall light. When he sought her eyes, however, they weren't focused on his face. They were open so wide that she was in danger of needing blink therapy, and they were peering at his chest.

"I don't think we should have this discussion until you put on your shirt," she said.

"I left it back at your parents' house."

"Why'd you do that?"

"Because you were so determined to get me alone that you didn't give me time to pick it up."

"I was not determined to get you alone!"

"Then what are we doing alone inside your house?"

She looked confused. Adorably confused. She blinked, shook her head, bit her lip, and ran a hand through her messy hair. He got a whiff of her strawberry shampoo. "Okay, maybe I did want you alone." Her voice grew sharp. "But it's not because of what you're inferring."

"And what am I inferring?"

"That . . . that I think you look good without your shirt on!"

"You don't think I look good without my shirt on?"

"Well, yes . . . I mean no . . . heck, I want to mean no."

He advanced a step and fastened his hands on her upper arms, admiring the spirited way she tried to defend herself against an attraction he was starting to think was invulnerable. Although he thought her beautiful, it wasn't solely a physical attraction. He was also drawn to the intricate workings of that mind of hers.

"Why don't you admit you're as attracted to me as I am to you," he said, staring down at her. "C'mon, Annie. You can trust me."

Both of her hands moved to his bare chest, and he wondered if she could feel the quick dance of his pulse. He leaned toward her, expecting to hear soft words of acquiescence. Instead, he got a hard shove. He stumbled and slammed against the wall.

"Hey," he protested. "What was that for?"

"For playing me for a fool," she said, anger once again sparking her eyes. "Trust you? Trust you? How in the dickens can I trust you when you lie to me?"

"Lie to you?" Now he was thoroughly confused. He straightened from the wall, absently rubbing the part of his back that had smacked into it. "I don't know what you're talking about. When have I lied to you?"

"You told me you didn't have time to date anybody. Yet a few hours later, you took Felicity Pomposity to dinner!"

Oh, Michael thought as relief stole through him. *That's what this is all about.* This he could explain.

"It wasn't a date."

"Don't you dare give me that, Michael Reeves.

When a man takes a woman to dinner, it's a date. Especially when the woman is seen flirting outrageously with him."

Michael didn't remember Felicity doing any outrageous flirting, but he took it as a good sign that Annie would be jealous if she had. He smiled. "You sound like you're jealous."

"Jealous! Of that witchy Felicity Pomposity!"

"Her name is Felicity McMann," Michael said, backing out of shoving range. He wasn't leaving himself vulnerable before he could explain why he'd taken the veterinarian to dinner. Especially because he didn't plan to explain until he got some answers of his own. "And she's not a witch. She's a sincere, intelligent woman you happen to be crazy jealous of."

"I am not jealous!"

"Then explain why you're so angry. Just last night, you tried to get me to believe you'd be happy if I went out with any single woman in Elmwood who breathed."

"But I didn't want you to go out with *her*." Tears sprang to Annie's eyes, and she swiped at them. "She's not just any woman. She's the woman who would rather euthanize a peregrine falcon than give it to me. And you knew that, Michael. You knew that, and you still went out with her."

She whirled and trod away on her heavy boots, leaving the foyer behind and crossing the living room. It was filled with comfortable furniture and decorated in earthy shades of green, rust, and brown that seemed characteristic of her personality. The heart-aching sobs coming from her did not.

Michael was positive that Annie didn't often give in to crying, but those were definitely tears streaming down her face. Worse, Michael had put them there. He followed her, dismayed that he'd been trying to get an admission from her before he made one of his own. He caught up to her halfway across the living room.

"Get away from me," she cried, but he caught her by the shoulders and turned her. She blinked rapidly in an effort to stop the tears, but they spilled onto her cheeks, where they flowed in thick rivulets down her face. "This is humiliating. Just get out of my house and—"

"Stop it, Annie." He gave her a little shake. "It's not what you think. I know how much you care about those birds, and I would never do anything to hurt you."

"Don't flatter yourself." Even though she was crying, her voice was tough. "We've already established you're not my type. You don't have the ability to hurt me."

Liar. Michael wanted to call her one, pointing to her tears as evidence that she cared at least a little. But first he had to make her understand why he'd asked out her enemy.

"The only reason I asked Felicity to dinner," he began, and her head dipped, as though she couldn't stand looking at him, "is because I wanted to talk her into giving you that falcon."

"What?" Annie's head shot up.

"That's one of my strengths, kiddo." He gently rubbed her shoulders. "I network with people, find out what they know, and get them to come around to my way of thinking. Didn't you say yourself that I was a slick talker?"

"I don't think so," Annie answered slowly, "but I would have if I'd thought of it."

Michael smiled, lifted one of his hands, and brushed the tears from her cheeks with his thumb. "Yeah, and I don't suppose you would have meant it as a compliment, either. But slick talking has its benefits. Felicity now understands you're educating people about wildlife. She also realizes a dead falcon wouldn't do anybody any good."

The hope that leaped into Annie's eyes was a wondrous sight to behold. It also made worthwhile the two excruciating hours he had spent listening to Felicity explain how to deal with injuries to various types of birds.

"Are you saying what I think you're saying?"

He wiped the rest of the tears from her cheeks. "Only if you think I'm saying you can pick up that peregrine falcon any time."

"Really?"

"Really."

She flung her arms around his neck so enthusiastically that it caught him unprepared. He lost his balance and went toppling backward. His back hit the floor with a dull thud, his body cushioning Annie's fall. For a moment, he couldn't breathe.

He felt cool hands on either side of his face and the nubby texture of the carpet against his back. Slowly, her face came into focus. This time, her eyes weren't flashing either anger or annoyance. They were warm, like the embers in a fireplace. And very concerned.

"Oh, my gosh," she said. "Are you all right?"

"I will be once you thank me properly," he said, rubbing the back of his head. "Knocking me over doesn't count."

"Thank you," she said. "I can't believe you did this. I only mentioned that I wanted that falcon one time."

"I know, and I've been beside myself worrying that you'll need something else for that menagerie of yours. A falcon I can deliver, but there might be a problem if you start wishing for an ostrich."

She laughed, a tinkling sound that softened her tough-girl image. "Even though you can't distinguish a raptor from a bird that lives in Africa, you are still the most amazing man."

"That's what I've been trying to tell you."

She touched his cheek and smiled at him. "I owe you an apology."

His gaze dropped from her gold-streaked brown eyes to her quivering mouth. It was a pretty mouth. Wide with full, rosy lips that promised paradise. "I'm thinking that just saying you're sorry won't be good enough."

The smile broke through. "And why might that be?"

"You have to admit that all those things you yelled at me were grievously unfair. That got me to thinking that, in the way of an apology, a deed might seem more sincere than words."

"A deed?"

"A kiss," he clarified, and traced her lips with his index finger. To his surprise, his hand was shaking. Come to think of it, his voice was shaky, too. "I'm thinking that getting that falcon for you is worth at least one kiss."

Someone screamed, although that wasn't the reaction he'd been aiming for. His mind was still muddled from the fall, but the curious part was that Annie's mouth hadn't opened. They looked at each other with puzzled eyes. Then a familiar voice resounded through the house, and they both understood too well.

"Christine, come quick! They're in the living room. She's tackled him and pinned him to the floor. I think she's hurt him bad!"

At the sound of Rose Kubek's hysterical words, Annie's body went still. Then she buried her face against his shoulder. Michael lifted his neck and peered around Annie's head. She was still on top of him, and they were lying with their feet pointed toward the entrance of the house.

There, at the head of the living room, stood Annie's mother and his own. Michael closed his eyes and wished them away, but they were still there when he opened them.

"Are you sure they're fighting, Rosie?" his mother asked in a whisper.

"I told you. She said she was going to break his perfect nose and knock out his perfect teeth. What else could they be doing?"

His mother tilted her head and regarded them consideringly. "Maybe they were kissing," she suggested.

Annie buried her face even deeper into his shoulder, but Michael had had enough. "Could we have a little privacy here? I'm fine."

His mother averted her eyes as though they really

had been making out on the floor. "Now that we've seen that Michael's okay, maybe we'd better leave, Rosie," she said.

"Leave?" Mrs. Kubek looked wary. "How can we leave? They shouldn't be doing this kind of thing until after the wedding, Christine. We can't leave them like that."

"What we shouldn't have done," his mother said, taking Mrs. Kubek by the hand, "was let ourselves into the house."

"But we knocked and knocked and nobody answered. And we had good reason to think Annie was attacking Michael. That's why I drove to your house to get you."

"Come on, Rosie. Let's get out of here." His mother gave Mrs. Kubek's hand a hard tug, and she finally gave in to her friend. Michael had never been happier in his life to see the backs of two women.

"I'll give you a call in fifteen minutes, Annie," Mrs. Kubek called over her shoulder. "We need to talk about how soon we can arrange the wedding. The sooner, the better, if you ask me."

Annie groaned, but she didn't say anything until they heard the door shut behind their mothers. Then she raised her head, revealing a face as red as a tomato.

"Now do you believe we have a problem?"

Chapter Nine

"Annie, would you stop looking over your shoulder? You have a very pretty neck, but it's difficult to carry on a conversation with it."

"Just a minute," Annie said as she continued her inventory of the other people in the dimly lit dining room. "I have to make sure there's nobody here we know."

"How could there be? You insisted we rendezvous at the corn field at the end of that country lane, and then we drove an hour to get here."

"I didn't want to rendezvous there," she corrected, still scanning the crowd. "I wanted to rendezvous here."

"Driving sixty miles at night in that pickup of yours

128

wouldn't have been too smart, Annie. It's not exactly the most reliable vehicle on the road."

"At least it's nondescript. Your car's so flashy, anybody could have followed us."

"In the highly implausible event that anybody would have wanted to follow us, you made sure they weren't by checking the rear-view mirror every couple of minutes."

"Somebody had to do it," Annie said. A diner a few tables away had a bald head with the same sheen as Uncle Frank's, but on closer inspection the wisps of remaining hair at his temples were red instead of brown.

"Then you insisted I park at the rear of the inn and asked the waiter for the most secluded table in the place. Not only that, you're dressed all in black. I swear, Annie, you're acting like we're on a reconnaissance mission instead of a date."

"I already explained that we can't be too careful. If my mother catches us together again, she might forget about the church wedding and haul us before the justice of the peace."

She interpreted his sigh as acknowledgment that they couldn't afford to make any more mistakes, but the scrape of a chair against the gleaming hardwood floors came as a surprise. So did the sight of Michael pulling her chair back from the table.

"If we change seats," he explained, "then you'll be able to see the rest of the people in the restaurant without turning around. And I'll be able to look at your face instead of that very pretty hair of yours."

As he talked, he reached out and touched her curls, sending delicious little sensations along her scalp and making Annie glad she'd taken the time to wash her hair after she'd left the park today. She didn't usually care how she looked, but she liked the gleam that came into Michael's eyes whenever she looked good.

She smiled at him, got up and settled into the seat he'd vacated. The flame on the candle in the center of the table flickered, casting golden light over his face. She supposed it was time to acknowledge that she had actually begun to like his too-perfect looks, from his outlandishly straight nose to his ultra-high cheekbones to his green-as-grass eyes.

His lips curved at the corners as he lifted his wine-glass, watching her over the rim as he drank. When he put down the glass, Annie had the inconceivable urge to run her fingertips over his lips. Then again, maybe the urge wasn't so inconceivable. She'd always loved his mouth.

"Am I dreaming, or do I actually have your full attention?" he asked, smiling all-out now. "Correct me if I'm wrong, but you're not examining the other diners anymore."

He was teasing her again, but his smile was so winning she couldn't seem to get upset about it. She smiled back at him. "I've already examined them. I figure we're safe, barring any unforeseen arrivals."

He shook his head at the same time he reached across the table and captured her hand. The lazy circles he drew on her palm with his thumb felt so good she didn't consider pulling it away from him. "This is crazy, do you know that?"

His eyes roamed over her face, as though memorizing every line. Annie's heart slammed into her ribs until it settled into a beat about twenty thumps a minute faster than usual.

"What's crazy?" she asked, although she was starting to think she was.

"Sneaking off so our mothers don't find out." He brought her hand to his lips and kissed the back of it. "It's not like I'm ashamed of this thing between us."

"What thing?"

He smiled and drew her hand all the way across the table so that it covered his heart. It was beating as furiously as her own. "This thing that makes my pulse jump whenever I'm near you," he said softly.

She didn't know whether his eyes softened as he made the admission or if it were a trick of the candlelight. She shakily withdrew her hand and put it in her lap, away from his reach. She couldn't think clearly when he was touching her, and, if she couldn't think, she couldn't talk.

"You shouldn't be ashamed of it either," he finished. "I don't want you to be ashamed of me."

"How can you think that? I'm not ashamed of you. You're great." The way his eyebrows raised at her compliment made her think she'd been too effusive in her praise. "I mean, in an okay sort of way."

He grinned. "If I'm so great, in this okay sort of way, you should think about openly dating me. This one clandestine meeting isn't going to be enough for either of us. I want to make the most of every minute we have left together. I think we should tell people about us."

"But my mother will make our lives a nightmare if we do," Annie wailed. "Did you know she actually called me at the park this morning to discuss china patterns? She wants me to register for bone-white china, because she thinks some of the patterns resemble uneaten food."

"Annie, we've already talked about this. I know your mother is a problem. So is mine. But they're problems we can get past. Nobody can force us to get married."

"My mother will try."

She looked so miserable that Michael sighed, which he realized he'd been doing a lot of around Annie. He'd been so thrilled when she said she'd go out with him that he'd agreed, against his better judgment, to pick her up in a corn field and drive her to a secluded, mountaintop restaurant.

Instead, he would have liked to show her off. Her black pants covered her fabulous legs and her silky black top was way too concealing, but she still looked fabulous. The dark color of the fabric contrasted nicely with her dewy skin and made her naturally rosy cheeks seem rosier. He even thought she'd enhanced her already-pretty lips with color. He certainly wanted to think she'd tried to look pretty for him.

"You can't imagine how irritating it is," Annie continued, "to have my mother and her minions butt into my business."

"Her *minions?*"

"Everybody else in town," Annie explained.

Michael chuckled, then put his hands up in front of his face. "What you're about to hear is an opinion.

Remember that if you don't agree with it. Just don't punch me in the nose."

Annie rolled her eyes. "I've curbed my pugilist tendencies since the other night." He lowered his hands, and she reached out and tapped him on the nose. "Besides, it would be a sin to mess with perfection."

"I thought you said it was too straight."

"It's a woman's prerogative to change her mind."

He traced his nose with his finger, only half-convinced she wouldn't lay one on him. "In that case, you should consider yourself lucky that so many people want to butt into your business."

"Lucky?" Annie's dark eyebrows rose. "If you lived here, you wouldn't say that."

"Oh, no? I've only been in Elmwood a week, and already I know how special it is. Do you know how rare it is to find a place where people are genuinely interested in you? Where you belong? I'm a military brat. I've never had that."

"Surely you have friends in California."

"I know people at the office, sure, but I don't know my neighbors. I could drop dead in my townhouse, and it'd be days before anyone found me."

"Then why do you stay there?" She put her elbows on the table and considered him, which hadn't been his intention. He wanted her to examine her life, not his.

"I don't think—"

"Why?" she persisted.

He let out a breath. He might as well state the obvious so they could get back to talking about her. "Because CompTech's there, that's why. Because it's where I need to be in order to become vice president."

"But why do you want to be vice president?"

Michael stared at her. Didn't she know anything about him at all? Didn't she realize the vice presidency was the driving force in his life? That he wanted to do as well in his career as his father before him? "Because I want to be a success."

"And you think a vice presidency is the measure of a successful life?"

The sardonic lift of her eyebrows made him forget the original point of their conversation. "Let me guess. You don't?"

She shrugged her slim shoulders. "Not if it doesn't make you happy."

"I'm happy."

Annie's lips twisted. "It sure didn't sound like it a minute ago when you talked about dying alone in your townhouse."

"Wait just a—"

"It sounded to me like you'd be happier living in Elmwood."

As soon as she said it, Annie knew that was what she wanted him to do. She still had no intention of marrying him, but two weeks of Michael Reeves would never be enough. He'd become a craving, every bit as intense as the one she had for the crisp, unpolluted air of the countryside.

"Elmwood?" He sounded shocked, as though the idea had never occurred to him. "Just because I like Elmwood doesn't mean I could live there. I have my career to think about."

"Oh, yeah. I forgot what your father the general always said. Success doesn't come to you. You have to chase it." Annie tried not to sound sarcastic, really she did. From the irritated look that marred his handsome features, she doubted she'd succeeded.

"What's wrong with chasing success?" he snapped.

"Nothing. Nothing at all," Annie said quickly. Now she'd gone and offended him, which wasn't what she'd intended at all. "Forgive me, Michael. I shouldn't have baited you. It's just that you and I have such different concepts of success."

"I shouldn't ask you what you mean, but I'm going to."

Annie sighed. How could she put this diplomatically? Since she didn't know, she didn't try. "Okay, it's this way. To you, the pinnacle of success is being paid a lot of money to be a principal player in a large, powerful organization. To me, it's good people, clean air, and countryside so beautiful that it makes me feel like weeping."

Michael rubbed the back of his neck as he regarded her. His perfect features contorted into a scowl. "You make it seem as though money and success are more important to me than anything else."

"Aren't they?"

"Ambition is not a crime."

"You're saying it's a virtue?"

"Yes . . . I mean no." He gazed at her across the table. His green eyes were troubled. "Heck, Annie. I don't know what I mean. How do you do this to me?"

"Do what to you?"

"Make me forget what I'm talking about," he said, his voice low.

A high-voltage current seemed to pass from him to her. She shifted in her chair and cleared her throat. This was such an important conversation that she didn't want their attraction to derail it, but she could see it was going to. She made one last stab at salvaging it.

"I don't think you forget," Annie said. "I just think you don't want to talk about it."

She was only half right, Michael thought. His goals were so firmly in place that he didn't want to examine his motives for reaching for them. Nor did he want to delve too closely into the reasons he was glad his mother had thus far rejected every person he'd tried to hire to help her, thus prolonging his stay in Elmwood.

But Annie was half wrong, too. His world had tilted on an axis the moment he'd walked into the Kubek home and met her laughing dark eyes. Since then, he'd had a devil of a time keeping anything straight.

Annie bit her lower lip. "Why are you holding my hand?" she asked.

Michael looked down, surprised to see that his large hand was covering her smaller one. He hadn't realized he'd reached for it. "I like holding it," he said, lifting his eyes to hers. The room could catch fire, and he wouldn't notice. He lowered his voice. "Don't you like me holding it?"

She nodded, making him smile. That was his Annie, honest to a fault.

"It's going to be hard to eat dinner this way," he said, whispering now.

"I don't think I care," she whispered back.

Annie leaned her head against Michael's and gazed at the shimmering sky of stars through the open sunroof of his Lexus. Her eyes filled with moisture and she surreptitiously dabbed at the corner of one of them with her fingertip.

"This is what you meant about countryside so beautiful that it makes you feel like weeping, isn't it?" he asked softly.

"How did you know I was?"

"I'm attuned to you, Annie Kubek. You talk tough, but I know about the soft heart that beats under that ranger uniform."

Right now, it was beating for him. After she'd stopped checking the front of the restaurant for her mother and her minions, the night had turned magical. Food had tasted better, firelight had glowed brighter, conversation had been more interesting—all because she'd been with Michael.

The magic had been so all-pervasive that they'd both wanted to prolong the evening. Annie had spied a turnoff during the drive back to Elmwood, and they'd ended up parked in a dark field gazing at the stars.

A gear shift was positioned between the bucket seats of his Lexus, but their heads were together, their hands linked. Who would have thought that they'd get along so exquisitely, that being with him would be so utterly perfect?

As if on cue, he turned his head so that their lips met in a soft, sweet kiss. When it was over, she smiled against his mouth and then into his eyes when he drew back.

"What do you think of me now?" he asked.

She smiled wider, not understanding why he felt the need to ask. Wasn't the answer obvious? "I think you're great."

"Great?" He cocked an eyebrow teasingly. "That's the best you can come up with?"

She smoothed his beautiful blond hair back from his fabulously high forehead. He was really the most extraordinarily handsome man. Now, she figured, was not the time to hold back the words pushing at her lips. So she let them out. "How about amazing, marvelous, sensational, phenomenal?"

"I like phenomenal," he said. "Definitely my kind of adjective."

She giggled.

"So I guess this proves I'm your type after all." His grin, Annie thought, looked triumphant. "You can't imagine how hard I've been trying to get you to eat your words."

Annie's body went still as she remembered telling him she made a better match with a barred owl than with him. He couldn't possibly mean what she thought he meant. A minute ago, it had felt as though their very souls had merged. Could she have been wrong?

"I didn't realize that's what you were trying to do." Her voice was low, but he obviously didn't hear the warning in it.

He laughed. "You're kidding, right? After you laid

down that challenge, I made up my mind on the spot to make you fall for me. Any guy would have."

Pain radiated through Annie, replacing the haze that had been obscuring her common sense. She jerked back from him and wrenched open the door of the car.

"Hey," he yelled after her as she started across the open field. Her high heels sank into the mud, and her ankle turned. It hurt, but not nearly as much as her pride. Tears pricked the back of her eyelids as she extracted the shoe from the mud. She'd been stupid, stupid, stupid.

Michael scrambled out of the car and chased after her. This couldn't be happening. One minute, Annie was exactly where he wanted her, cuddled against him, as content as a cat. The next, she was as angry as a tigress.

"Wait a minute," he called. "What did I do?"

"What did you do? How can you even ask that?" She kept walking as she railed at him, not bothering to turn. He wondered where she was going. "And to think I trusted you. I should have known I can't trust anybody but myself. But no . . . I had to let myself get blinded by your bloody perfection."

"Annie," Michael said sharply, finally catching up to her and putting a restraining hand on her shoulder. She whirled, but the eyes that met his were damp with tears. For the first time, he considered that something other than anger might be making them so.

"I can't believe I let myself walk into your trap. I should have known you only gave me the rush because of those things I said." She blinked. A few tears escaped and fell down her cheeks, breaking Michael's heart. "I should have known you were only avenging your bruised male ego."

What she was saying sunk into Michael's brain. For the first time since she'd gotten out of the car, he was able to breathe. He gave her a little shake.

"Annie, that's not how it is."

"Don't you dare lie to me," she shot back, her tears falling in earnest now. "I was there, Michael. I heard what you said. You wanted me to eat my words. That's what this is all about."

"That's not what this is about." Michael leaned toward her until his face was just inches from her. "Sure, I wanted to hear you say you were wrong about me."

She made a half-hearted attempt to get away from him, tearing at Michael's heart, but he wouldn't let her go. He couldn't let her go. Not until he explained.

"But I also want you. I've wanted you since I saw you last week. Heck, maybe your mother is right. Maybe I've wanted you since the day we were born." He stopped, cleared his throat, and wiped at her tears with the pad of his thumb. "You're all I think about, Annie. All I dream about."

She blinked rapidly, slowing her tears. She raised her watery eyes to his, and, in that moment, he saw that she believed him. He also saw something else, something that heated his blood and warmed his heart. He wasn't alone in what he was feeling. She felt it, too.

She rolled her tear-dampened eyes. "It's not enough that you look as perfect as you do," she said tartly. "No. You even have to make perfect apologies."

He grinned, put his hands under her arms, picked

her up, and whirled her around. She laughed through her tears.

"Michael Reeves, you put me down right now."

"Not until you say I'm forgiven," he said, laughing up at her.

"You're forgiven," she yelled halfway through another whirl. When she was thoroughly dizzy, he put her down and kissed her. She wrapped her arms around him, and it felt as though she were enveloping every inch of him in hope, in warmth, in love.

"Ah, Annie," he whispered against her lips. "I think I'm falling in love with you."

Later, as he drifted off to sleep beside her as they gazed at the stars, he wasn't sure if he'd said the words or only thought them. The only thing he was sure of was that he meant every word.

A series of shrill chirps intruded on Annie's sleep. She shut her eyes tightly, unwilling to leave the warm cocoon which encased her mind and body. The mysterious chirping, however, wouldn't stop, leading to a terrible thought.

What if the chirps were coming from a baby bird separated from its mother? What if Mrs. Death or Maltese, her new falcon, had hatched a baby that needed help? The thought snapped her eyelids open.

She wasn't anywhere near the raptor mews, but in the bucket seat of a Lexus parked in a green, tree-dotted field. Dawn was breaking, telling her she and Michael had fallen asleep in his car. The chirps were coming from the pocket of his jacket.

"Michael," she said, nudging him. He stirred and

murmured her name. A luscious thrill ran through her, followed by more chirps. Darn that infernal thing.

"Michael," she said, louder this time. He opened one eye, which looked very green in the soft light of dawn. "Would you answer your cell phone?"

"Cell phone?" he asked, adorably confused. She couldn't help it. She kissed him, then figured she better chastise him to even things out.

"If we're going to keep hanging out," she said in a warning tone, "you're going to have to turn it on vibrator mode."

He answered the phone. "Oh, hello, Mrs. Kubek. How can I help you?"

Mrs. Kubek! Coming fully awake, Annie sat up straight in the bucket seat and turned to him in horror. How could he have given her mother his cell-phone number? She looked down at her wristwatch, which showed the time as just past 6:00. What was her mother doing paging him at this time in the morning?

She made furious hand signals, trying to alert Michael that he was not, under any circumstance, to tell her mother she was with him. But he wasn't paying her any attention. He was listening and nodding, his face grave.

"Calm down, Mrs. Kubek. I understand how frightened you've been, but you don't have to worry any longer. She's perfectly safe."

Annie's stomach clenched. If she weren't trying to be completely silent she would have screamed a warning. She pressed her palms together, prayer-style. *Please,* she prayed, *don't let him slip up.*

"How do I know she's perfectly safe?" he asked.

Please, she prayed, *make up a lie. Any lie.* "Because she's right here with me."

In abject misery tinged with unmatched horror, Annie covered her eyes.

"No," she heard Michael say. "I don't think she does want to talk to you."

He paused and, just when Annie thought things couldn't get any worse, they did.

"How do I know? I don't think she's a morning person. She just woke up, and she seems a little grumpy."

Chapter Ten

"I can't believe you're still upset about this." Michael glanced at Annie, then returned his attention to the bumpy dirt road. The edge of the corn field where Annie had left her pickup the night before came into sight, but he wasn't yet ready for her to get out of the Lexus. "Don't you think you're blowing it out of proportion?"

He took another quick glance at her, just in time to catch the incredulous look she shot him. He felt ridiculously glad that she'd met his eye. The rest of the drive, she'd kept her forehead pressed against the window as she stared at the passing scenery. The bond they'd formed during their date seemed to weaken with every mile they'd traveled.

"I mean, what was I supposed to do?" Michael

asked. "After that farmer found your pickup and called her, your mother was frantic. She thought you'd been kidnapped. What was I supposed to tell her when she asked if I knew where you were?"

"You could have made something up. You didn't have to tell her I'd just woken up!"

Michael grimaced. She had a point there. He shouldn't have said that. He wouldn't have if Mrs. Kubek hadn't been sobbing hysterically and he hadn't been awakened from a deep, satisfied sleep.

"But Annie, it was perfectly innocent. We fell asleep in the car, in separate bucket seats," he said as he pulled his car to a stop. The day was lovely, with the sun shining down so gloriously onto the corn field that it resembled a shimmering sea of green and gold. Life would be perfect if only she'd smile at him.

"Okay, I admit I shouldn't have said that. I made a mistake."

"I'll tell you what was a mistake." Annie opened the car door and got out. "You and me."

Panic rose in Michael like the ocean at high tide. He rushed out of the car and positioned himself in front of the driver's door of the pickup before Annie could reach it. Her hair curled about her head every which way, wrinkles creased her jet-black outfit, and her makeup had worn off. A wave of longing hit Michael hard. She looked every bit as good right now as she had the night before.

"You can't mean that, Annie. Last night was pretty terrific. You know it every bit as much as I do."

She put her hands on her hips and gave another of

her patented glares. "Thanks to you, so does my mother."

"So what?" Michael had been trying to be the calm, sensible one, but he couldn't manage it any longer. He lost the rein he'd been holding on his temper. "I don't understand why it matters if she knows."

"I already told you why it matters." Annie shouldered past him and pulled open the door of the pickup. "She's been driving me crazy for twenty-five years, telling me I'm going to marry you. Now that she knows we were together last night, she'll make my life a nightmare."

Michael squeezed in between the pickup and the door before she could shut it. She turned her blazing eyes on him, eyes so beautiful that in them he found the answer to their problem. He was surprised he hadn't seen it before.

"Then move," he said, biting his lip before he completed the rest of the sentence and threw her into another tizzy. Suddenly, it was all so clear. He didn't want her to move just anywhere. He wanted her to move to Los Angeles. With him.

"Move?" Incredulity replaced the angry misery in Annie's expression. "Why on earth would I move away from Elmwood?"

"Because your mother, and everybody else in town, make you miserable by butting into your business."

"You just told me last night how lucky I was to have people butt into my business."

That was true. But last night, Michael didn't have an agenda. Today, he did. "The result's the same: you're miserable."

"I'm not miserable. I'm . . . frustrated. But that doesn't mean I could move away." The anger had drained from her, and he suspected she knew they were talking about much more than geography. She reached out and touched his cheek. "My life's here, Michael. My birds are here. I'm a small-town girl who wouldn't be happy living anywhere else."

Her words sliced through Michael like a finely sharpened knife. It wasn't as though he hadn't expected them. He knew her life was in Elmwood with her large, wonderfully annoying family and her raptors just as his was in Los Angeles at CompTech. But hearing her say she'd never move hurt. He reached out, took her hand, and brought it to his lips.

"I'm sorry I slipped up when your mother called," he said, still holding her hand. "The last thing I want is to make things difficult for you."

Annie squeezed his hand and gave him a tremulous smile. "I'm sorry, too. Sometimes I let my temper carry away the rest of me."

Michael smiled. "I guess this means we don't have to sneak around anymore."

Annie bit her bottom lip. "I don't know, Michael. I mean, what's the point? It's not as though you're staying in Elmwood. In a little while, you'll be—"

He lowered his head and kissed her, stopping the rest of her words and savoring the sweetness that pervaded his soul. He cupped her head, enjoying the little sounds she made deep in her throat as they lost themselves in each other. When he drew back, her lips clung to his for a moment. He traced them with his fingertips.

"That's the point," he said, his voice low. "I promised Joe I'd help him design software after he gets off work today, but I can meet you after that."

"I can't," Annie said, and there was genuine regret in her voice. "I want to, but I have some things I need to take care of. I probably won't get home until ten or eleven."

"I guess coming by your house then is out of the question?" Michael asked, hoping she'd contradict him.

"If you did, tongues would be flapping in Elmwood," Annie said. "And I'm not ready for that."

"Tomorrow, then?"

"Tomorrow." Annie sealed her promise with a kiss.

When she drove away, he stood in the middle of the dirt road, staring after her. He wondered how he was going to get through the years without her when his heart screamed a protest at the prospect of a day apart.

"You're sure you want to wait to tell me what you're bursting to tell me?" Annie asked the next evening as she and Michael walked up the sidewalk to her house. Early evening had settled on Elmwood, darkening the sky to a bluish gray. The streetlights glowed yellow, but Annie's house was dark. "I swear, you've been jittery since you picked me up at the park."

He linked his hand with hers and swung it in a high arc. "I can tell you over dinner."

Annie laughed. "Think again, Buster. You haven't

tasted my cooking yet. Dinner might kill you. Now what is it?"

He stopped, turned to her, put his hands on her shoulders, and smiled into her eyes. Enthusiasm brimmed from him, almost, but not quite, obliterating the disappointment that had nearly crushed Annie since she'd seen him last.

"Remember how I told you Joe and I were going to work on designing software last night?" Michael barely waited for Annie to nod before he continued. "I had a brainstorm right in the middle of it." He squeezed her shoulders. "What if we design software educating schoolchildren about raptors? Think about it, Annie. It would be perfect. You could provide the material, Joe and I would do the designs, and everybody would win. You'd be teaching children and getting publicity for your center at the same time. You'd never have to worry about losing your birds again."

Annie's heart fell like a boulder in her chest. It was bad enough that she'd had her own dreams smashed. Now she was going to smash his.

"Too late," she said, trying to keep the hurt out of her voice. She'd cried enough tears last night that she almost succeeded. "I already lost them."

"You what?"

"That was why I couldn't meet you last night. We had a staff meeting to discuss budget cuts, and I made a last-ditch attempt to save my raptors." She grimaced, remembering the impassive way Lou Spinelli had stared at her while she made her presentation. "They didn't stand a chance."

"Why didn't you tell me about this meeting?" His

eyes bored into hers, and she could have sworn she saw hurt swirling in them behind his compassion.

"Why should I have? What does it have to do with you?"

Michael's mouth dropped open. "How can you ask that, Annie? What concerns you, concerns me. Maybe I couldn't have helped, but I certainly would have tried. You're the one who says I'm good at schmoozing. Maybe that's what it would have taken to save your birds. It got you your falcon, didn't it?"

Annie's spine stiffened, and she backed away from him. "I didn't need your help before, and I don't need it now."

He came forward a step. "I think you do. I think you're tired of playing the lone park ranger."

She shook her head. "Don't do this, Michael. I *won't* need you. I've gotten along without you for twenty-five years. When you leave next week, I'll get along without you for the next twenty-five."

Before the tears pricking the backs of her eyes fell, she spun around and walked to her front door. How had she let this happen? She'd known all along that Michael was all wrong for her, and here she was on the verge of bawling because he was set to leave her. Where was her stiff upper lip? Where was her self-respect? Where was her cotton-picking brain?

She pushed open the door, aware from the way the hairs stood up on the back of her neck that Michael was following her, and flicked on the lights.

"Surprise!"

Annie took a step backward, colliding with Michael's chest. His arms immediately came around her, and she was so shocked at what she saw that she let them stay there.

Every corner of her small house was filled with smiling, laughing people. Grandma Kubek had her mouth open and her teeth, thankfully, in place. Cousin Ursula of the frizzy hair was bouncing on the balls of her feet. Her mother and Michael's mother had their arms linked. Light momentarily blinded her, and she realized it was the reflection off Uncle Frank's balding pate. She twisted her head to look at Michael.

"It's my birthday tomorrow," she said by way of explanation.

Shouts of congratulations came from the crowd, which Annie thought was strange considering the occasion. Sure, turning twenty-five was a milestone. But, face it. If you looked both ways before crossing the street, it wasn't too difficult to reach the quarter-century mark.

He tightened his arms around her and smiled into her upturned face. "It's my birthday tomorrow, too. I didn't realize our birthdays were the same day."

"Same day, same year. That's one of the reasons our moms think we're meant to be together. If you don't believe me, ask my mother," Annie said. Michael's arms around her felt so good that she had to make an effort to use her long-suffering voice. Their mothers were walking their way, making it easier. Too late, she imagined the picture she and Michael presented, standing so close together.

"Unhand me. Now," Annie whispered desperately.

"Unhand you?" Michael's tone was light and amused. "What are you? A Victorian maiden?"

"Our mothers," Annie hissed, trying not to move her lips. Grandma Kubek had waylaid them, giving her a few more precious seconds to get away from Michael. The trouble was, he was going to have to do the work, because she couldn't make herself move out of his embrace. "Our mothers are coming."

He whispered in her ear, ruffling the hair at her temple and setting off a torrent of shivers inside her. "Even if the British were coming, they couldn't get me to unhand you. Besides, it's a little late to pretend indifference now."

Their mothers, having resumed their relentless march, reached them seconds later. Mrs. Reeves beamed. "We're so very happy for you."

Hmmm, Annie thought. Maybe turning twenty-five was a bigger deal than she thought.

Her mother's smile wasn't as wide as her friend's, but it was apparent. She'd found a dozen little ways to let Annie know she didn't approve of an unmarried couple spending the night together. As Annie had predicted, she didn't believe that it had been an innocent night. "I'm glad things are working out, even if you two have jumped the gun."

Before Annie could say that it was her mother who'd jumped the gun—after all, their birthdays weren't until tomorrow—Aunt Eugenia rushed forward. The vertical red stripes in her canary yellow dress matched the swipe of lipstick on her teeth. She missed her lips so often that Annie made a mental note to buy her a magnifying mirror.

"You two make such a cute couple," Aunt Eugenia

gushed. "I told your Uncle Janos after Walter's wedding, Annie, that you picked yourself a fine *kochanie*."

"But he said he'd be *my kochanie*." Grandma Kubek had sidled up beside them. She took a look at Michael and broke into gales of hysterical laughter.

"Just what exactly does *kochanie* mean, Annie?" Michael asked, a question he should have followed up on at the wedding. He'd started to, but something, probably Annie's beautiful dark eyes, had distracted him.

"Sweetheart," Annie answered. Those eyes, those gorgeous eyes, were looking up at him now. "It means sweetheart."

"Well, in that case," he said as Aunt Marta brought out her accordion and launched into a polka, "how about a dance, *kochanie?*"

Annie's Uncle Frank let out a lusty yell that might have been the Polish equivalent of "yee-ha," and Michael spun Annie through the house while all the people who had come to celebrate their birthdays cheered.

She laughed, matching him step for step, making him glad the party had distracted her from her misery over losing her raptors. Because she wasn't going to lose them. He'd see to that. He wished he'd known about the meeting so he could have put the rescue plan he'd devised in motion sooner. But it wasn't too late to do some fast talking and reverse the damage.

He gave Annie another twirl just before they would have bowled over the living room sofa, complete with her magazine-reading father. The birthday crowd broke into applause for their nimble feet.

As Annie's laughing eyes met his, he remembered

what he'd told her at the restaurant. That she was lucky to have so many people who cared about her. She smiled at him. For a moment, before he remembered that he was going to have to give up Elmwood and Annie way too soon, he felt like the luckiest son-of-a-gun in the world.

Breathless from dancing, Annie collapsed into the sofa in her family room and smiled as Grandma Kubek claimed Michael for another go. People were all around them, paper plates balanced on their laps, munching on the kielbasa her mother must have cooked up that afternoon.

She leaned her head back on the sofa cushions, and her eyes fell on the print of a pair of soaring falcons she'd had framed for her parents. With their wings spread and talons extended, they were stunning in their beauty.

Her mind ricocheted to Maltese, the injured falcon that had just arrived at her raptor mews. What would become of him and the rest of her birds now that Lou Spinelli had disbanded her program? Would they be shipped off to the rehabilitation center to be euthanized?

Tears sprang to Annie's eyes, and she wiped them away. She would not think about her birds now. Tomorrow would be soon enough to mourn the death of her program. After all, Michael would be gone before her birds.

For now, during this short time when they were together, she was going to enjoy the sight of him whirling her grandmother around the house. Michael caught her eye, grinned at her, and gave the laughing Grandma Kubek a twirl. *Oh, my.* Grandma had her teeth out again.

"I've never seen Michael so happy." Christine Reeves, dragging her heavy cast along, dropped onto the sofa next to Annie. "He's always so busy working that he never takes the time to enjoy himself."

"That can't be entirely true," Annie said as Michael executed a deft athletic move that put his body between her grandmother and the nearest wall. Whoever had laid out her house hadn't meant for the polka to be danced through it. "I've seen him play basketball. Nobody gets to be that good without practicing."

"Oh, he practiced all right. His father, rest his soul, insisted on it," Mrs. Reeves said on a sigh. She peered at her. "Has Michael told you much about his father?"

"Only that he was a general in the Air Force and that he wanted Michael to chase success."

"That's the sanitized version," Mrs. Reeves said, her expression pensive. "My husband was a good man, right up to the moment he dropped dead of a heart attack when he was fifty years old. I sometimes think the reason he died young was that he drove himself so hard, always striving to make the next officer rank and the higher pay grade.

"He drove Michael hard, too. Oh, I probably shouldn't have let him, but Michael excelled at whatever he did. It seemed harmless to let his father push him to make the highest grades in his class. To be the best player on the basketball team. To reach for the most prestigious jobs." She bit her lip. "But now I think it wasn't so harmless."

Annie stared at Mrs. Reeves long and hard, trying to pick up her hidden meaning. "You think the vice presidency isn't something Michael wants as much as something he thinks he should want?"

"I'm afraid so. Don't get me wrong, dear. Michael loves working with computers. But I've never heard him talk as excitedly about CompTech as he does those software programs he and Joe are designing." Mrs. Reeves smiled and put a hand on Annie's arm. "And I've never seen him look at a computer the way he looks at you."

She closed the space between them and planted a soft kiss on Annie's cheek. "Thank you, dear. Until he met you again, I thought Michael might never figure out what was really important in life. Thanks to you, I can forgive myself for doing what I did to get him to Elmwood."

Annie started to ask what she'd done to bring Michael to Elmwood, but the first half of her sentence made even less sense than the last half. She focused on that. "What did Michael figure out was important when he met me?"

"Love," Mrs. Reeves said simply, as though it were the most obvious answer in the world. "Love is what's important."

Annie was just about to correct Mrs. Reeves's misconception when her mother, carrying a champagne glass, burst into the room. In a mystifying move, she climbed on top of an ottoman so she was poised above the crowd.

"Silence, please," she yelled in such a commanding voice that all conversation came to an abrupt halt. All eyes turned toward her. She raised the champagne glass high. The half-smile she'd been wearing earlier that evening had turned as broad as the mouth on one of those smiley faces that adorned T-shirts and coffee mugs. "I'd like to propose a toast."

As if by magic, several of Annie's relatives appeared. Some handed out plastic champagne glasses while others poured the bubbly liquid into them.

Annie searched the room for Michael and found him holding two full champagne glasses. Their eyes met, and he headed straight for her. He handed her a glass, sat down beside her and put his free arm around her. Annie snuggled against him as she waited for her mother's pronouncement.

She'd probably make a big deal over Annie and Michael sharing a birthday, maybe even attributing it to fate. Last week, talk like that would have sent Annie stewing. But with Michael's arm securely around her, Annie found that she couldn't get worked up. About her mother, at least.

"I'd like to propose a toast," her mother said again. "To Annie and Michael."

"To Annie and Michael," the crowd parroted.

Her mother's smiling eyes focused on them. Her voice rang out strong and clear. "May your lives be long and your love be strong."

Their love? Annie glanced at Michael, who looked as confused as she felt. First Mrs. Reeves, now her mother. Why was everybody talking about love? And quite suddenly, even before her mother muttered the hated D-word that had haunted her throughout childhood, she knew.

"And may the *destiny* that brought them together decree that they always be as happy as they are today. On this, their engagement day."

Michael fingers tightened around his champagne glass at Mrs. Kubek's unfathomable proclamation, cracking the plastic at the same time Annie's glass slipped from her fingers. Within moments, the fronts of both their trousers were soaked.

Engaged? Had Mrs. Kubek actually said they were engaged? He was dimly aware of Annie's bald-as-an-egg uncle letting out another ear-splitting yell and her aunt cranking up the accordion for one more polka. His glazed eyes focused on Mrs. Kubek, who downed the champagne in a single gulp and hopped off the ottoman. She set down the glass and reached for his mother's hand.

"We did it, Christine," she yelled. "We helped destiny along."

"Yes, we did," his mother said and laughingly went along as Mrs. Kubek spun her around the room.

If Michael had commanded the ability to speak at that moment, he might have warned Mrs. Kubek to be careful of his mother's broken leg. Instead, he watched in mute silence as his mother clunked around the room like a plaster prancer.

Then an incredible thing happened. The cast, the one he had been so solicitous of for the past week, fell off and clanked to the floor. And his sweet mother, the one he'd thought couldn't possibly be in on any sort of pact, kept dancing!

Which meant two things: that her leg wasn't broken and that Annie had been right the entire time.

They'd been set up by a scheming pair of women who'd betrothed them in infancy. His shocked eyes met Annie's as hands patted him on the back and voices rang out with congratulations.

He recovered the ability to speak first. "We need to do something," he said, which was all the impetus Annie needed. She gave a determined nod, sprang up from the sofa, and took his hand. Annie climbed onto a sturdy wooden coffee table, and Michael followed suit when she tugged at his hand.

"Attention," she yelled when they were standing head and shoulders above the crowd. Nothing happened. Her relatives and friends kept dancing, and the accordion kept playing. She implored him to help with a look, then counted to three.

"Attention," they yelled on cue. This time, the music stopped. This time, the crowd focused on them and went deadly silent.

"There's been a mistake," Annie began.

"Annie and I," Michael continued, "are not now, nor ever have been, engaged."

If possible, the silence in the room grew thicker. A sea of shocked eyes stared back at them, and for long moments nobody said anything at all.

"*Nie rozumiem.*" Annie's Grandma Kubek spoke into the silence. She was mumbling because she still hadn't put her teeth back in, but Michael had picked up enough Polish during the past week to know she was saying she didn't understand. She cocked her white head. "Don't you love each other?"

Michael waited for Annie to hotly refute what her grandmother had suggested, but instead she said nothing at all. She looked at him, evidently as incapable of denying that she loved him as he was of saying he didn't love her.

"Love," Michael said, once more looking out at the crowd, "has nothing to do with it."

"Nothing at all," Annie seconded.

After a few more moments of uncomfortable silence, he was aware that all eyes in the crowd had dropped and were focusing on their hands, which were tightly linked.

Annie had evidently noticed the same thing, because, at the same moment, they both released their grip on one another. Their hands slid apart, slowly, so that their fingers disengaged one by one until only their pinky fingers were touching. Then they, too, came apart.

Chapter Eleven

Annie kicked at a stone, careful not to aim it at her raptor mews and frighten the inmates. She watched it disappear into the grassy underbrush beneath the trees and wanted to follow suit. Or better yet, burrow in the dirt like a mole.

Life, she thought, was cruel.

It wasn't enough that she was set to lose her beloved raptors. Oh, no. The same fate over which her mother was always rhapsodizing had dealt her another, far greater blow. It had made the only man she'd ever love an ambitious technophile who thought he belonged in the concrete jungle. And it was sending him back to that jungle today.

Annie kicked at another stone. Blast Michael's mother for not being able to pull off the Deception of the Cast for at least another week or so. Annie no longer cared that her mother and Mrs. Reeves had conspired to bring her and Michael together. She only cared about having more time with him and knowing she wasn't going to get it.

Love, she thought, was heartless.

Here she was, ready to suffer through a lifetime of her mother's I-told-you-sos for the love of a man, and he was leaving on the next plane.

She couldn't even take consolation in the fact that her mother would have to eat her words, because she and Michael weren't destined for each other after all. What fate in its right mind would pair a park ranger with Cosmopolitan Man and expect it to work out?

"Hoot, hoot."

She looked up to see Mr. Hoots hopping over to the edge of the cage and stopping. He stared out at her with his big, round eyes, and for a crazy moment Annie thought she saw sympathy shining through them. As though Mr. Hoots had gotten over his jealousy of Michael and was aware that her heart was cracking.

"Hoot, hoot," the owl cried again. She advanced toward the cage, crouching down beside it.

"Hi, big boy. You're a doll to be worried about me, did you know that? Yes, you are. It's good to have a friend at a time like this."

The owl was looking at Annie so trustingly that fresh pain assailed her. How was she going to stand losing her raptors? Worse, how was she going to protect them? She'd telephoned every zoo and park system in a three-hundred-mile radius, and none were equipped to take them. Michael had promised to stop by before leaving for the airport, but now she almost hoped he wouldn't. She could only take so much pain in one day.

"Happy birthday, Annie."

The deep, rich voice that sounded from behind her was unmistakably Michael's. She loved the sound of it. When he was gone, she was sure she'd hear it in her dreams.

She got to her feet and turned, savoring the tall figure Michael made. The late-afternoon sun lit his blond hair and highlighted his sculpted features. He was as turned out as always in pleated navy-blue slacks and a kelly-green polo shirt that made his eyes glow vividly green.

No man had ever looked so good, so perfect, so absolutely right for her.

On closer inspection, however, she noticed his eyes were undercut by circles and the cast of his mouth was drawn. She wanted to fling herself into his arms, cover his delicious mouth with kisses and assure him that things were going to work out between them. But she couldn't, because they weren't going to.

When he got on that plane and flew away from Elmwood, Michael would be as lost to her as her birds. A sob rose in her throat, but she cut it off before it escaped.

"Happy birthday, Michael."

He took a step forward, then another, feeling as though she were a human magnet drawing him to her. Then he forced himself to resist the pull of her allure and stop.

After the party had come to an abrupt end the night

before, they'd agreed to slam the brakes on their relationship. They both knew that every minute they spent together would make it that much harder to split apart.

She started to kick at a stone with one of her booted feet, then seemed to have second thoughts. Her eyes, like his, were droopy and sad, as though she hadn't gotten any more sleep than he had. He felt like he should do something, like serenade her with the "Happy Birthday" song, but he didn't much feel like it.

Only a foot or two of space was between them, but Michael felt as though they were separated by an invisible wall neither dared cross. Behind her, he could hear her birds stirring and see Mr. Hoots watching their every move.

"Are you very angry with your mother?" she asked, catapulting his thoughts to the night before when his mother's cast had clanked to the floor, taking his happiness with it. He'd known, at that moment, that he had to leave Elmwood straight away. His mother no longer needed him to find her a caretaker, and it was imperative that he get back to CompTech and make up for lost time.

"How could I be angry at her when what she did brought me here to you?" Instead of making a smart-aleck response, like she would have only last week, Annie's hand went to her heart. He tried to make the corners of his mouth lift, but instead felt them drooping. "For the record, you were right about the pact and the betrothal. She confessed everything, right down to the pinky link."

Annie nodded. "My mother said they were sure they were doing the right thing. That, even back then, we looked at each other like we were in love."

Their eyes locked, and, for a moment, Michael felt dizzy.

He blinked and cleared his throat. "How's your mother taking it?"

Annie rolled her eyes, warming his heart. She loved her mother as much as he did his, but Annie wouldn't be Annie if she didn't complain about her mother.

"I never knew people really wailed and ground their teeth until last night. Such histrionics you've never seen. She can't believe she was wrong. And you know how hard-headed she can be."

This time he did smile. Like mother, like daughter.

He watched as she reached into the pocket of her ugly park-ranger trousers, which he still resented for covering her fabulous legs. She pulled out a package no bigger than a ring box and held it out to him. "I got you a birthday present."

"You did?" He advanced toward her, mustering all his will to grab the package and not her. He un-wrapped it in record time, revealing a beautifully crafted lapel pin.

"I figured you were so natty, you probably liked things like that."

He took the pin out of the box and turned it over, examining it. It was fashioned of pewter and showed a great bird with its wings spread and its talons low-ered.

"It's a peregrine falcon. You got me one, so I'm returning the favor." She looked down at the ground and scuffed her feet. "I thought it might be something to remember me by."

"Oh, Annie," Michael breathed, no longer able to keep from touching her. He gathered her into his arms, where she went willingly, buried his face in her short, dark curls and smelled strawberries. "I love it, and I love that you thought to get me it. But I don't need anything to remember you. You're in my heart to stay."

His heart thumped so loudly, he thought it might scare her birds. "I don't know where I'm going to get the strength to leave you," he said into her hair.

"When do you have to go?" she whispered.

"In a little while." He drew back and looked down into her face, memorizing every endearing line. Leaving was the only logical choice, he knew that, but it was so darn wrenching. He should turn around and not look back. But he couldn't. Not yet. Not until he'd done what he'd come to do. "I got you a birthday present, too."

As if on cue, bright, young voices sounded from the surrounding parkland. In a moment, a heavyset middle-aged woman came into view. Following her were a dozen small children, skipping and laughing and creating a ruckus. Michael reluctantly disengaged himself from Annie and turned toward the advancing woman and her pixie-sized army.

"Hello, Mrs. McGillicutty," he called to her. Her plump face creased into a grin, and she waved.

"You got me Mrs. McGillicutty for my birthday?" Annie asked in wonder. Michael laughed.

"No, silly. Mrs. McGillicutty teaches kindergarten

at Elmwood Elementary. I told her you'd be happy to tell her students about your raptors." He whispered in her ear, enjoying her look of bemusement. "Your birthday present isn't here yet."

"Is this the lone ranger?" Mrs. McGillicutty asked as she walked up to them.

"The park ranger," Michael corrected, running his hand lightly down her arm before making the introductions. Pride swelled at him at how Annie quickly adjusted to the situation, as though a surprise visit by a class of kindergartners was an everyday occurrence.

"Go ahead and start, Annie," Michael said, excusing himself. "I need to check on something."

Annie watched his retreating back, wondering what he was up to. Even though she knew he wasn't yet leaving for good, she wanted to call him back, wanted to beg him not to go. Then two dozen eyes focused on Mr. Hoots, who was hopping around the cage as though in the throes of a comedy routine.

"Hoot, hoot," he cried, and childish giggles filled the air. "Hoot, hoot."

Annie turned away from Michael, toward the children, and launched into her program. Fifteen minutes later, she was still talking. The children, incredibly, were still listening.

"Can I hold the Vulcan, Miss Annie?" A little pig-tailed girl piped. With blond hair and green eyes, her coloring was similar to Michael's. Annie's heart was heavy. If things had been different, she and Michael could have had a child who looked like this.

"He's a falcon, honey, not a Vulcan," Annie said,

wondering if the girls' parents were *Star Trek* fans. "And holding him would be a very bad idea."

"Then can we pet him?"

Annie scooted down beside the girl and pointed toward Maltese, who was perched on a tree branch. "See his talons." All eyes went to the falcon. "They're sort of like our toenails, except they're very, very sharp. Like knives. Imagine how it would feel to pet a knife."

"Ouch!" a dark-haired little boy cried, and all the children giggled. The light-hearted mood continued for a few more minutes until Annie finished her program. Her thoughts immediately turned back to Michael, and she found him standing off to the side of the clearing next to a nicely dressed man she didn't recognize.

"Annie Kubek, I'd like you to meet Steve Granger," Michael said as he stepped forward with the other man.

"Steve Granger!" Annie exclaimed. "As in the director of Calvert County parks?"

"The very same," Steve Granger said, extending his hand. Annie took it, hardly believing that the parks director was here, in the flesh. She'd repeatedly called his secretary, begging to speak to him about her raptors, but had always been told he was unavailable.

"You can't imagine how glad I am to meet you, sir," she said, pumping his hand. He took it back, rubbing it slightly.

"Not half as glad as I am to meet you, young lady." Granger smiled. "I had no idea how worthwhile your program was until Michael here came to my office and invited me to see you in action."

"You went to his office?" she asked Michael, but Granger didn't give him time to answer.

"I'm very impressed with the work you do here," Granger said. "The way you made learning about raptors fun for the children was a joy to watch."

Annie's eyes again went to Michael, but he was backing away. He gestured to his watch and blew her a kiss that landed on her heart and stuck. Annie read his meaning perfectly. He'd miss his plane if he didn't leave straight away. Tears threatened, but she blinked them back.

"When that little girl asked if she could give the wings from her Halloween costume to Mr. Hoots to help him fly, I knew you had them hooked," Granger continued as Michael walked farther and farther away from them until Annie could no longer see even his retreating back. "Imagine an owl dressed in Tinkerbell wings."

The praise flew over Annie's head as she tried to make sense of what was happening. Michael was leaving, but he'd left something important behind. Somehow, she needed to piece together the events that had brought Steve Granger to the park so she could figure out what it was. "Did you say that Michael came to your office?" she asked.

Her question seemed to get through to him. He nodded. "Without an appointment, yet. He couldn't reach me by phone, so he practically forced himself into my office. I have meetings all day every day, you see, but he wouldn't talk no for an answer. He told me about the educational software your brother is designing and persuaded me to come out and see you. He said something about it being your birthday today."

Suddenly, everything clicked. Michael had accomplished what she hadn't been able to. He'd put Steve Granger, the one man in the county park system who wielded the most power, in a position to save her raptors. Steve Granger was her birthday present.

Gratitude welled in her like rising flood water as she realized what an amazing thing Michael had done for her. She wanted to wrap her arms around him and never let him go.

But she couldn't, because he was already gone.

"It hasn't been a very happy birthday," she confided, hardly daring to hope that Steve Granger would say the words that would rescue her beloved birds from certain death. "Surely you've gotten Lou Spinelli's recommendation that the raptor mews be disbanded."

No sooner had she said his name than Lou came into sight, accompanied by two men Annie recognized from the raptor rehabilitation center. Lou slowed when he spotted Steve Granger, but then walked confidently forward.

"Mr. Granger," he said, shaking the other man's hand. "To what do we owe this surprise?"

"Why are these men with you, Lou?" Annie interrupted before Granger could answer. Lou flicked her an annoyed glance, and she got a whiff of the wintergreen gum he chewed, before bestowing his insincere smile on Granger.

"This is Ed Hardaway and Johnnie Jericho from the raptor rehabilitation center," he explained, not looking at Annie. "As you probably know, Mr. Granger, budget cuts make it impossible to keep the raptor mews in operation. These men are going to see about removing the birds."

"You mean euthanizing the birds," Annie cut in bitterly. Lou looked at her as though she were an insect he wanted to brush off his arm.

"Must you be so dramatic, Annie?"

"Is this true?" Steve Granger's eyes went wide. "Did you actually authorize that funding be cut off to her raptors and that they be euthanized?"

Lou's chin went up. "Yes, I did."

"That's a terrible idea," Granger said, making Annie's heart jump with joy.

"With all due respect," Lou said, his chin quivering, "I'm in charge of this park, and I know what I'm doing."

Granger extended to his full height, and a steely determination cloaked his face. "With all due respect, I'm in charge of the people who run all the parks, and I disagree. In fact, I think it would be better to transfer you from this park than to move Ms. Kubek's birds."

"Do you mean it?" Annie asked, letting out the breath she'd been holding. "Can the raptors stay?"

"I always say what I mean," Granger said, and Annie waited for the euphoria to overtake her. But a strange thing happened. Instead of feeling euphoric, she felt deflated. What should have been one of the happiest moments of her life had turned into one of the saddest.

The reason hit her like a punch to the heart. Michael

wasn't here to share it with her. Michael. Who she couldn't live without.

She'd been such an idiot, stubbornly insisting that they hadn't been born for each other, that she hadn't told him she loved him, hadn't begged him not to go. So now he was leaving Elmwood, and her, for good.

Annie simply couldn't let that happen.

"I'm sorry, but I've really got to go," Annie told the two men. In record time, she was behind the steering wheel of her pickup, listening to the fruitless sounds of an engine that wouldn't turn over.

"Blast," she said, striking the wheel with the palm of her hand. She'd been so hard-headed that she hadn't listened to Michael when he told her the engine needed to be overhauled. So hard-headed she hadn't listened to her heart, either. She got out of the pickup and hurried toward the nature center when she saw Lou Spinelli coming toward her. His face was flushed red with anger.

"You're not going to get away with this, Annie," he said through clenched teeth, shaking a finger. "I don't know who you think you are, but—"

"Give me your keys," Annie interrupted, authority ringing in her tone.

"What?"

"I said," Annie bit out, *"give me your keys."*

A confused look crossed Lou's face an instant before he reached into his pocket and pulled them out. Annie didn't give him time to think about what he was doing. She snatched them from him and watched him swallow his gum. Then she ran to his car.

She was inside with the engine running before he

got to the driver's side window. "What are you doing?" he yelled as she pulled out of the parking lot.

"What does it look like I'm doing, Lou?" Annie called out the window. "I'm commandeering your car."

Annie heard Lou let loose a string of epithets as the back tires of his car spun on gravel and she shot out of the parking lot, but her mind was already on Michael.

Two hours and two wrong turns later, Annie left Lou Spinelli's car in the loading zone of the Pittsburgh airport and sprinted into the terminal. *Please,* she prayed, *please don't let his plane be gone.*

She checked the nearest overhead computer screen for flight departure times and found that only one airline had a plane bound for Los Angeles in the right time frame. Unfortunately, the plane was due to leave any moment.

She ran to the gate listed on the screen, losing precious seconds as she went through the security checkpoint. She arrived breathless and panting just as the big plane backed away from the gate and taxied down the runway.

"Can I help you, Miss?" a pretty blond asked as she approached the passenger-service desk.

"Yes, can you check to see if Michael Reeves was on that flight?"

"Reeves," the woman said as her manicured finger ran down a list of names on her computer screen. "Yes, Michael Reeves had a ticket for that flight. Is there anything else I can assist you with?"

Behind her, through the large glass windows, Annie

could see the silver plane rising into the sky, taking the man she loved with it. Quite suddenly, a decision that would have been unthinkable only a week before, became inevitable.

"Yes," Annie said, her mind made up. "I need to get on a plane to Los Angeles."

The woman smiled. "How soon do you need to go?"

Annie made some calculations and named a time much later that evening. "I have to go home and pack," she explained, then looked down at her clothes. "Not to mention change."

Quite suddenly, she wanted to be wearing something besides her park-ranger uniform when she saw Michael again. Considering how much he liked her legs, maybe she'd even put on the flirty sundress her sister had sent for her birthday.

Annie would have tugged on the skimpy strap holding up the bodice of her sundress if she hadn't been so busy throwing clothes haphazardly into the open suitcases on her bed.

The prospect of leaving Elmwood shot daggers of pain through her heart, but she ignored them. She knew now that a place, no matter how ideal, could never replace the man she loved. No wonder her sister had left Elmwood to marry her husband. No wonder Christine Reeves had traveled from military base to military base.

Love made sacrifice worthwhile, even desirable.

Living in Los Angeles wouldn't be easy, but Annie could get a job there. Surely they had parks in Los

Angeles. Maybe, and about this she was doubtful, they even had one large enough for raptors.

Even if they didn't, she could stand anything as long as she was with Michael. Even concrete. At the thought of him, a wave of longing so intense hit her that she imagined him standing at the doorway to her bedroom.

She drank in the lovely sight of him, from his blond hair to that delectable mouth on which she'd developed an unquenchable fixation. Then she blinked, resigned to having the mirage disappear. Except he still stood there in the doorway.

"Michael," she breathed, and his name caught in her throat. Tears of gladness sprang to her eyes, blurring her vision. One question was paramount in her mind, but she could barely form it. "What are you doing here?"

His beautiful mouth smiled and his green, green eyes traveled down her body, roaming over the legs she'd left bare for him. "You left your door standing wide open, so I let myself in. I hope you don't mind."

Mind? How could she mind when she was willing to go to Los Angeles, or even Timbuktu if it came down to it, to be with him? She stood rooted to the spot, afraid he'd disappear if she moved. Afraid it was all a lovely dream.

"Of course I don't mind. I meant what are you doing in Elmwood? I thought you were on a plane to California."

The answer filled Michael with awe. He'd been so busy the last few hours, checking every street in Elmwood searching for the car she'd hijacked from Lou

Spinelli, that he hadn't taken the time to think about the decision he'd reached.

"I've been looking for you," he said, stalling. She was staring at him with saucer-wide eyes in which he saw his future, and, amazingly, she was wearing a pretty yellow dress baring her arms and legs. "I think I talked your boss out of filing charges that you stole his car, but I'm not real sure about that."

"He might not be my boss anymore. Besides, it can't be stealing when he gave me the keys," Annie said. She caught her bottom lip between her teeth, preventing him from being able to tell if it was trembling. "You didn't answer my question. Why are you still in Elmwood?"

Michael was about to respond when he finally spotted the open suitcases on her bed. Could they mean what he thought they meant? Was such a thing possible? "Why are you packing?"

"Why do you think I'm packing?" If it hadn't been for the sudden moisture in her eyes, he would have thought she was annoyed with him. "I was coming to Los Angeles."

"You were?" What she said didn't make sense. Annie was to Elmwood what falcons were to flight, what vultures were to road kill. Unless . . . "Did Steve Granger give your program the ax after all?"

"No." Annie shook her head. "Thanks to you, he's determined to keep it running."

"And you were still going to leave? Why?"

Annie's teeth released her lip, which noticeably quivered. The tears he'd thought he saw in her eyes brimmed over and fell down her cheeks. "Because you don't live in Elmwood," she whispered. "You live in Los Angeles."

He smiled, a slow grin that started with his lips and finished in the depths of his eyes. "Let me get this straight. You were going to leave Elmwood for me." His laugh began deep in his throat and erupted.

She put her hands on her hips, dashing away the tears from her cheeks. "I fail to see what's so funny."

"Oh, Annie," he said, closing the distance between them, putting his hands on her shoulders and looking down into her tear-streaked face. In her luminous brown eyes, he saw everything he never knew he wanted. "You can't leave Elmwood for me, because I'm leaving Los Angeles for you. Weren't you listening when I said I couldn't make myself get on the plane?"

Her breath hitched. "But what about your vice presidency?"

He amazed himself by laughing at the very thing that he'd thought he most desired. "To heck with the vice presidency," he said with asperity. "A vice presidency can't keep me warm at night. It can't laugh with me, love with me, and bear my children." He held her at arm's length and did an exaggerated sweep of her body with his eyes. "A vice presidency wouldn't look nearly as good as you do in a dress."

She blushed through her tears, making her look better. "What are you saying, Michael?"

"I'm saying that everything I need is right here in Elmwood," he said as the truth of the statement struck him with wonder. "There's your brother, who says he'd be delighted to start a software-design business with me. There's your wonderful, wacky family. And there's all the nosy townspeople who make me feel like I truly belong."

He lowered his voice, and it trembled with emotion. The next few moments were the most important in his life, because the woman he was holding was infinitely more precious than a job could ever be. "But most of all, there's you. I love you, Annie. I love you so much I think it must have started back in the crib, when our mothers say it did."

Annie's laugh sounded like something between a hiccup and a sob, and tears freely ran down her face. "So do I," she said. "But even though I love you so much it hurts, I might have to kill you if you tell my mother that."

Laughing, he gathered her to him. Their mouths found each other and they drank deeply of each other's souls.

"I'd ask you to marry me if I didn't think you'd say no," Michael said long moments later, his forehead resting on hers.

"Who says I'd say no?" Annie shot back.

He lifted his head. The tears were gone, and Annie, his Annie, the one who'd charmed him from the moment she'd looked at him and burst out laughing, was back.

"You," he said, grinning at her. "I distinctly remember you saying you'd rather marry a barred owl than me."

"That was before I'd seen you play basketball."

He laughed. "In that case, will you marry me?"

"You were taking so long about it," she said, giving

one of her patented eye rolls, "I thought you'd never get around to asking."

"Annie?" His tone held warning.

"What?" Hers had asperity.

"You haven't answered."

She harrumphed. "I love you, don't I?"

"Yes, you do."

"Our birthdays are on the same day, aren't they?"

"Yes again."

"And we've been betrothed from infancy."

"You've got me there."

"Then what answer except yes would make sense? Of course I'll marry you." Her eyes danced. "The sooner, the better."

As he kissed her and the familiar thrill coursed through him, Michael thought their mothers surely must have been right.

They really had been born for each other.

Epilogue

Christine Reeves and Rose Kubek, their hands clasped and their mouths curved in identical smiles, stood in unison as the organ launched into the music signaling the bride and groom should exit the church.

Annie, radiantly beautiful in a pearl-encrusted white gown, held onto the arm of her new husband, who was resplendent in a black tux. The were gazing into each other's eyes as though they were alone in the church.

"I'm so glad Michael talked Annie out of wearing a frilly white pantsuit." Rose dabbed at her moist eyes with the tissues she'd used throughout the ceremony. "She looks so much prettier in a dress."

"She loves him, and he loves her," Christine said simply, sighing with contentment as they followed the throng of people parading out of the church behind the newly married couple. "I've never seen a couple so right for each other."

A young woman wearing a turquoise dress stepped out of the aisle a few pews ahead of them and a few paces behind Annie's younger brother Joe. Rose clutched at Christine's arm. "Who's that?" she asked, pointing to the dark-haired woman.

"Oh, that's my niece Carla. She's from my husband's side of the family. Remember Cecilia, John's sister? That's her daughter. She's visiting from Philadelphia."

"Is Carla single?

"She is."

Rose clapped her hands. "That's a very unusual color she's wearing. Ever since he was a baby, Joe's been partial to that exact shade of turquoise. Do you know what this means?"

"I'm almost afraid to ask," Christine said.

"If an eligible woman comes to a wedding wearing a dress of an unusual color and it happens to be the favorite color of an eligible man in attendance . . . well, that's destiny at work."

Christine screwed up her face. "Are you sure? I've never heard that one before."

"Of course I'm sure. Trust me. My son and your niece, they're destined for each other." She put her graying head next to her friend's. "Now all we need do is figure out a way to get them together."

"Oh, all right," Christine said. "But if there's any broken bones involved, this time you're going to fake it."

A little while later, after the guests had gone through the receiving line, the bride and groom emerged to a shower of bird seed. Overhead, in the cloudless azure sky, a pair of falcons flew over the festivities.

Annie and Michael didn't notice. They held out their hands to each other, smiled, and made a promise even more sacred than the one they'd taken in church.

They linked their pinky fingers.